THE SYMBOL SEEKERS

ALSO BY A. A. GLYNN

The Case of the Dixie Ghosts
A Gunman Close Behind
Mystery in Moon Lane

THE SYMBOL SEEKERS

A. A. GLYNN

WILDSIDE PRESS

*For my niece, Julie and great niece Quinn with love; and
to the memory of Michael Burgess (Robert Reginald)
in deep appreciation of his encouragement.*

Published by Wildside Press LLC.
www.wildsidebooks.com

CHAPTER 1

THE BOX AND MR. O

The beam of the shaded bull's eye lantern swung around the darkened room. Where it smote the walls it showed richly patterned wallpaper and, here and there, it fell upon ornaments that spoke of a collector of good taste. It came at length to a wall bearing several framed portraits, all of a distinctly American character. There were George Washington, Benjamin Franklin and Jefferson Davis, President of the Confederate States of America which, nearly two years before this February of 1867, were defeated after four years of bloody civil war with Abraham Lincoln's United States.

Curiously there was a portrait of Maximillian, the puppet emperor of Mexico, set up by the French after a reckless and ill-fated invasion. The light moved down and found a table, laid out as a kind of naval shrine. It bore a couple of models of men in naval uniform, a pair of antique pistols and a spyglass. Lastly, it picked out a long wooden box, fastened by solid looking brass locks.

One of the two burglars working in the dark whispered excitedly in an unmistakable Liverpool accent:

'That's it! Grab it, lad and let's get out of here, quick.'

The pair were professionals and they were doing a professional job of burglary in this comfortable villa in Birkenhead, across the River Mersey from Liverpool. The owner of the residence, a distinguished American whose name was honoured around the world, and his family were sleeping soundly upstairs, totally unaware of the larceny in progress below them.

Charlie Sephton and Bill Twist were physically and morally stunted products of the tangle of cramped streets and alleyways surrounding the docks of the great seaport in Northwest England. They had been recruited by a mysterious man known as "Mr. O" to break into the villa and steal the box they had just located. The pair showed him the most grovelling deference when in his presence but, privately, Charlie Sephton called him 'the fella from London', while Bill Twist called him 'the Dago' by reason of his slightly olive skin and his vaguely foreign manner. He had offered the two thieves the high sum of five pounds each when the box was delivered to him.

Sephton and Twist had broken in by expertly forcing the window of this room As usual, they had planned their thieving expedition well, using all their criminal cunning. Behind a bush in the garden, they left certain "props" that would aid their return across the river to Liverpool with the box they were about to steal.

Sephton took the box from the table, found it to be heavier than he thought and tucked it under his arm. Then, moving swiftly and silently, the pair made for the window and climbed out into the fairly spacious garden. The very first signs of dawn were beginning to signal a new day as the pair slipped behind the evergreen bush that offered a screening barrier of thick leaves where other shrubbery was in a state of winter nudity. It was there that they had left the articles of disguise to aid their getaway. There were a couple of battered buckets some cans of paint and brushes; a pair of smocks as worn by workmen, liberally splattered with old paint; a pair of caps, also paint-splattered and a large sheet of the kind used by painters to protect furniture. Bold as brass, the pair left the scene of their crime by the garden gate in the guise of painters with Sephton carrying the box, wrapped in the sheet, under his arm.

They had pre-planned this departure carefully, so that, after walking for some distance through this more genteel district, they were soon close to Birkenhead's docks where streams of workers were gathering in the vicinity of the Liverpool ferry boats.

Many residents of Liverpool worked in Birkenhead and vice-versa, so this gathering and mingling of both sets of passengers on the landing stages was a regular event of the working day. In an era when working people commonly wore the garb of their calling day in and day out and policemen and soldiers were compelled by law to do so, two men garbed as painters among a crowd of genuine daily toilers were likely to be taken without question for what their clothing declared them to be.

The Liverpool bound vessel was waiting to take passengers on board when Sephton and Twist arrived at the landing stage. A chilly wind, polluted by the smoke and odours of dozens of riverside industries was blowing off the river and a dock police-man in tall hat and blue tunic was standing at the bottom of the gangplank, swinging his arms to stimulate his circulation.

As Sephton and Twist joined the stream of passengers shuf-fling up the gangplank, they passed him and he cast his eye over the gear they carried, including the sheet concealing the long box under Sephton's arm.

'Off to do a bit of painting, lads?' he asked.

'Yeh, some offices in Dale Street,' responded Bill Twist without batting an eye.

'Good thing you'll be working indoors,' said the good na-tured policeman. 'I reckon we'll have rain later, if not snow.'

Shuffling on up the gangplank, the two burglars exchanged sly smiles at having smuggled the stolen box past the limb of the law so easily. On the open upper deck, crowded with work-ers because its accommodation was cheapest, they sat with a group of genuine toilers. Each took out his British working man's comforter, the clay pipe, lit up and smoked contentedly throughout the short passage in spite of the river wind.

When they arrived on the Liverpool side of the river, they had more good fortune in not being challenged by those known in their social circles as "scuppers"—policemen—of whom there were many on duty and, once they were out of the dock gates, they hastened through streets of old houses whose charac-ter became increasingly sinister the deeper they penetrated the district.

They came to a narrow street of frowning old houses where they climbed the broken steps and entered the ever open front door of one known as Ma Sugden's Boarding House—in reality, a sailors' doss house. They entered a sparsely furnished front room which had been exclusively reserved for them. There, they dumped their painting gear, took off their smocks and Sephton placed the box, still wrapped in the sheet on the scarred table in the middle of the room.

They sat in two rickety chairs and waited.

'D'you reckon he'll come?,' asked Bill Twist.

'Course he'll come,' said Sephton. 'Why would he put up the job then welsh on us?'

'Dunno, except he's a Dago and you never can tell what a Dago will do,' replied Twist.

'You're being illogical, lad,' scorned Sephton. 'The fella from London wants that box—or whatever's in it—badly. Besides, he's paid Ma Sugden for the use of this room. He'll show up all right.'

'I'd like to know more about him,' commented Twist. 'He takes good care we never learn his proper name or where he really comes from.'

This was true. Mr. O burst into their lives having tracked them down to the Mermaid and Flagon, a dockland tavern that was their regular drinking den. He was all aristocratic style, making it plain that he considered himself to be far above a pair of Liverpool "scallies" such as themselves. He proposed the theft of the box from the home of the distinguished American exile and offered a price. The three met again only twice to iron out the plan, the rendezvous being pubs in different parts of Liverpool where they were unknown.

The canny Mr. O admitted he was from London but from which part he never said. Nor did he ever disclose how he'd heard of the two provincial thieves but they were highly flattered by news of their fame reaching the capital. From the street outside Ma Sugden's Boarding House, there came the jingle of harness trappings, the clip-clop of a horse and the grind of iron-rimmed wheels on hard cobbles.

'It's him—coming in a cab!' declared Bill Twist.

From beyond the window came a hoarse command to stop from the cabby to his horse and, a couple of minutes later, Mr. O entered the room. He was tall and well turned out in a black winter topcoat and a top hat and gloves and he carried a black, silver headed stick. As soon as he entered, Sephton and Twist, drilled in the slavish subservience the English lower classes were expected to show to those who considered themselves to be their betters, immediately stood up. Each whipped off his workman's moleskin cap.

Mr. O had a thin wisp of a light coloured moustache which, with his olive skin strengthened the suggestion of foreign origins. Another alien touch was the scent of Turkish cigarettes that came into the room with him. Although cigarettes were brought to the notice of the British smoking public more than a decade before when British troops fighting in the Crimean War adopted them from their Turkish allies, they never fully caught on. The stolid British smoker might concede that, remembering the privations and shortages the troops had to endure in the Crimea, it was understandable that they would accept anything that could be smoked when the Turks made the comradely gesture of offering their cigarettes. But the only proper smoke for an Englishman was his traditional pipe or cigar.

Mr. O, however, seemed to be addicted to cigarettes. He smoked them with a quick, nervous sucking action as if hungry for nicotine. Even before offering any greeting on entering the room, he produced a case from which he took a cigarette. He lit it with a flint and wheel lighter. Then his only greeting was a curt nod to his small, undernourished partners in crime.

'Did you get it?' he asked.

'Yes, sir. There it is, on the table,' said Charlie Sephton.

'Any trouble with the police?' asked O, walking to the table. He picked up the box and unwrapped it from the sheet.

'No, sir. Everything went as clean as a whistle,' said Sephton.

'As clean as a whistle, sir,' echoed Twist, thinking that emphasising the criminal skill of his partner and himself might induce O to increase their reward.

Surrounded by a haze of cigarette smoke, Mr. O examined the brass locks on the box. 'No sign of a key, I suppose' he commented.

'No sign, sir,' said Sephton.

'No matter. It can be put right easily enough. The price we settled on was five pounds each, I think?' said O.

'Yes, sir,' said Sephton and Twist in unison and with enthusiasm.

From his pocket, O produced a soft leather bag fastened with a drawstring. From it, he took a number of gold coins and placed them in two small piles on the table. Remembering the instructions of their youth, emphasising that they should show some decorum in the presence of their betters, the pair tried to avoid looking like birds of prey swooping on carrion when they grasped the coins and pocketed them.

Mr. O stepped back towards the door with the box in his possession.

'You'll be going back to London, I suppose, sir,' ventured Sephton.

O looked at him imperiously. 'I shall and that's as far as I intend to discuss this little adventure of ours,' he responded curtly.

He opened the door and left with a trail of perfumed smoke lingering behind him.

There was such a note of finality about his departure that Sephton and Twist felt they would never see "the fella from London, the Dago", again.

But it hardly mattered. He had left their pockets heavy with gold!

CHAPTER 2

A PAIR OF CONVERSATIONS
AND NO SALE FOR MR. O

Septimus Dacers chuckled. 'My dear Miss Van Trask, you do have a lively imagination—lady detectives, indeed!'

Miss Roberta Van Trask, frowning only slightly, looked at him coolly.

'It does not surprise me that you are scornful,' she said levelly. 'I fear you are a typical man and always ready to laugh at a new idea if it is put forward by a lady. Well, I believe ladies could bring some special talents to police work. Has it never occurred to you that because of her sex, a lady can go into places a man cannot go? Disguised as a female servant, perhaps; or maybe as woman shop assistant. If there were need to deal with small children, it seems logical that a lady would be preferable to a frightening male with a face full of whiskers and a shouting voice. I fear we ladies will never reform you men. You will always consider us to be your inferiors.'

'You do me an injustice,' Dacers objected. 'I do not consider you or any lady to be inferior to men. I have the greatest admiration for feminine intelligence and ability...it's just that there is so much rough and tumble in tackling crime that it is—well it's—er—just not a ladylike business.'

'Tosh, Mr. Dacers,' Miss Van Trask said, almost in pity. 'You are just like the bulk of men—totally hidebound in your view of women.'

The sunshine, remarkably strong for early February, streamed through the tall window of the breakfast room of Carrington's Hotel, close to the United States' Embassy in Grosvenor Square, London, where Miss Van Trask's father, Theodore Van Trask, was a senior officer under US Ambassador, Charles Francis Adams. It touched highlights to the silver teapot, and the china on the table at which the couple sat. It gave an enhancing emphasis to the delicate beauty of Miss Van Trask's face, framed in the halo of her bonnet and the inner rim of neatly dressed dark hair. Together with her sparkling blue eyes, it brought out one of the many attributes of this young American woman that fascinated Septimus Dacers: the hint that a lively, tomboyish spirit of adventure danced just beneath her calm and dignified demeanour. Doubtless it was this that prompted her to mention that she would quite like to be a detective, which caused Dacers to laugh.

He was a private enquiry agent, so called because the official police did not like such functionaries calling themselves detectives. His laughter set off one of their spirited discussions, a feature of their weekly breakfasts.

'Mr. Dacers, you claim detective work is not ladylike and you talk of rough and tumble. Well, I think you'll agree that there was a great deal of extremely nasty rough and tumble in our Civil War, so recently ended,' she said. Her long residence in Washington, DC, cheek by jowl with the State of Virginia, had given her speech the soft and warm cadences of the American South. 'Well, Clara Barton was inspired to leave comfortable government employment in Washington and, without any training, to take up caring for the wounded, learning as she went along. Why, when attending to a wounded man on the battlefield, an enemy bullet ripped her dress and killed her patient. She didn't run away screaming; she simply moved on to the next man who needed attention. Now, she's revered in America just as your own Florence Nightingale is revered here. She inspired many Northern women to follow in her footsteps and there were plenty of Southern women who did the same thing. The battlefield hospitals were dreadful places, soaked in blood and filled with men suffering from the most grievous wounds. I suppose you'll tell me it was unladylike for those women to take up such work.'

Dacers, felt his defences falling under her attack and was beginning to regret his typical mannish reaction to her contention that there was a place for women in police work. He liked her fighting spirit and the way she stood her ground in an argument, He liked the emphatic way in which she stated her case, with her blue eyes flashing earnestly but otherwise without any emotion. He didn't even mind that she usually beat him with her logic.

There were many things about Roberta Van Trask that attracted Septimus Dacers. Indeed, he felt more than attraction. The plain fact was that he loved her. It was, however, an unspoken love. He was older by a few years and he mentally magnified the point, believing that if he proposed marriage, she would reject him, seeing him as almost an old man.

Now, on the point of conceding defeat in a verbal clash once again, he said: 'Miss Van Trask, I have told you I have nothing but admiration for women and their courage and devotion. In so many ways they shame us men. It is not the women of the world who take to the musket and the cannon to settle big differences. They understand too well the sorrow war brings. Why, I even think women should have the vote. Mr. John Stuart Mill is soon to bring a Bill before Parliament, calling for female suffrage. I feel he is right, though many are laughing at him. With some female influence in government, I'm sure there would be more humane laws in the land.'

'Yes, and perhaps more scope for womankind to enter the professions and trades', she said.

'I agree. If we do reach the remarkable point of having ladies in the House of Commons and the House of Lords, who's to say we will not have ladies keeping the Queen's—or perhaps King's—peace as detectives and policemen?'

'Police*women* if you please, Mr. Dacers,' she corrected, smiling. 'Police*women!*'

'Well, if it comes to pass let us hope it does so when the present crinoline craze is over,' Dacers said. 'Our lady constables would have a hard time of it chasing fleet footed felons if attired in anything so highly attractive but so utterly illogical as the creation you are sporting this morning,'

The regular weekly breakfasts which gave Dacers and Miss Van Trask the opportunity for the semi-serious conversations in which they scored points off each other were initiated by Miss Van Trask's diplomat father.

In 1863, while the Civil War was raging, Theodore Van Trask, a widower, was based at the London embassy while his daughter was in the Union capital, Washington, in a government office. When her father became seriously ill, Roberta decided to cross the ocean to nurse him. Although at one point, her father came close to death, he eventually made a good recovery and was able to return to his duties.

When Theodore Van Trask was required to go to Liverpool, a hotbed of support for the enemy of the United States, the Confederate States of America, hosting such activity as the secret building and commissioning of ships to attack United States' shipping. The US embassy engaged Septimus Dacers to accompany him as bodyguard. Dacers was known as an intelligent and discreet agent and this assignment caused a strong friendship to be forged between the diplomat and himself.

A little later, after Roberta and Dacers had figured in an affair that came to be called the Case of the Dixie Ghosts, Theodore Van Trask, realising that his daughter spent much time in their home and knew few people in London, devised the weekly breakfast at Carrington's for her and Dacers. At first. Roberta was accompanied by her black maid and companion, Esther. On rare occasions when his duties permitted, Van Trask also attended. After a while, Roberta told Esther she need not attend the breakfast if she did not wish to. Esther felt relieved because Theodore Van Trask was so rarely there that she was beginning to feel a gooseberry when at table with only Roberta and Dacers. She also had the distinct feeling that, strictly proper and almost puritanical though he was, Theodore Van Trask was playing the matchmaker when he set up the breakfasts for his daughter and Dacers...

The meal over, Dacers escorted Miss Van Trask to her home near Grosvenor Square, so short a distance that no cab was required and it was refreshing to walk in the crisp February air and the winter sunshine that gave some promise of spring. When the couple parted Dacers went in search of a cab to reach his Bloomsbury lodgings. Opening the street door with his key, he entered and found his landlady, Mrs. Slingsby, in the hall.

'Ah, Mr. Dacers,' she said 'breakfasting with Miss Van Trask again?'

'Yes,' said Dacers.'

'And how is the young lady?'

'Very well and she sends you her best regards, Mrs. Slingsby.'

There was a certain twinkle in Mrs. Slingsby's eyes. She was not an inquisitive woman but she had a romantic heart. She had no great wish to lose Dacers, her long established and valued lodger, but if she did, she hoped it would be to what she called "a nice wife". She had great hopes of Dacers and the American girl.

She indicated the hall table. 'A letter came for you this morning, Mr. Dacers,' she said.

He took the letter upstairs to his rooms and found it to be accompanied by a most acceptable cheque in payment for an assignment in which he nipped in the bud a cunning method of fraud operated by a few employees of a small building society. If not stopped in its early days, it had the potential to ruin the company. The letter was one of effusive thanks from the company's directors.

He took down his ledger from a shelf and entered the cheque. Then he checked the ledger to gather some idea of his finances. They were healthy enough but this year of 1867 was just opening and there was no telling how his fortunes would fare in the coming months. This train of thought led to a consideration of his chances of marriage to Roberta Van Trask, provided she accepted him—and provided he plucked up the courage to ask her. Earning his living on a catch-as-catch-can basis, could he ever afford to marry her? He thought not.

Then came the usual march of gloomy reasons why she would never be his bride. When she attended embassy functions on her father's arm as his companion, she must meet many young men whose eyes she must dazzle: trade emissaries, youthful military and naval attaches and the like. Any one of them might whisk her off to the altar. Then came the gloomiest of all: Roberta would laugh off his proposal because she considered him to be too old. No, she would not laugh; her nature was too compassionate for that. It would be a gentle, kindly rejection, but a rejection just the same.

He sighed and picked up the morning paper which, as usual, Mrs. Slingsby had left in his rooms. He took in some of the major stories.

There was much excitement at the opening of the latest great wonder of the world, the Suez Canal and a long article on what it meant for world trade. There was a bloody clash between Caucasian and Chinese miners on the Crocodile River gold diggings in Australia.

Nearer home, there was news of increasing fear of the Irish nationalist movement, the Fenians, furthering their aims by military action against Britain. Many Irishmen with Fenian sympathies had served in the armies of the American Civil War and now posed a threat, returning to Europe equipped with military experience which they were ready to use against British rule in Ireland. It seemed a fever of fear of the Fenians was gathering in parts of England.

From America also, more violence was reported from the agonised Southern United States: rioting ex-Confederate soldiers shot dead by Union troops in Texas; a party of freed slaves murdered in Virginia and masked riders in Mississippi burned down a plantation mansion acquired by opportunists who came from the North to snap up the property of ruined Southerners. Such opportunists were called "carpetbaggers". In this instance, after the burning, the carpetbaggers were hanged.

Because of his association with Theodore Van Trask and his daughter; his assistance to the US Embassy and the affair of the Dixie Ghosts, Dacers had found himself growing increasingly interested in American affairs, tangled though they were in this fraught post-war period when the fighting had by no means stopped.

He found himself reflecting on what he knew of the strife across the Atlantic which looked as though it was gathering pace.

It resulted from the policy of "Reconstruction", by which the victorious Northern States attempted to pacify their recent enemy, the South and bring it back into the Union of States. Harsh methods were used. The Union's new President. Andrew Johnson, who had been Lincoln's vice-President and who was tainted by a reputation for drunkenness, negated Lincoln's hopes for the moderate treatment of the vanquished South uttered only hours before his murder. Lincoln's call for malice toward none and charity for all was forgotten after that cowardly act which shattered the soul of the United States.

Johnson and his Radical Republican faction who held sway in the US government wanted punishment, so the South came under an iron grip with a virtual new civil war breaking out. Ex-Confederates fought the US military; carpetbaggers came in to plunder; freed slaves, cut loose from the old plantation life they had known, were offered scant protection and were burned out of such schools and churches as were set up for them. There were shootings and hangings in the dead of night. Then came fierce Southern riders, masked and mostly former Confederate cavalrymen who destroyed property acquired by Yankee incomers and, frequently, destroyed the incomers themselves. Eventually there emerged a powerful band of hooded, vengeful riders, robed in white to represent the ghosts of the Confederate dead and oddly named the Ku Klux Klan.

Genuine peace and national unity under one flag seemed as far away as ever, Dacers thought, as he folded the paper to lay it aside.

As he did so his eye caught a coded item at the bottom of a column of public announcements:

'LUB: The good father is wrong. The ban not con. Mtg to be arr—watch here. Si Se Ty'

Dacers read it once then a second time. He translated a small portion of the code with ease but the rest was meaningless. He did not know why but sight of the item brought to mind the American affairs he had just been thinking of and the case of the Dixie Ghosts, in which a set of confidence tricksters sought to make their fortunes with a spurious plan to restart the American Civil War.

All that morning, the notice, the code and the echo of the Dixie Ghosts affair persisted in coming into his mind.

Earlier that day, at just about the time Dacers and Roberta Van Trask were crossing swords in their semi-serious way over breakfast, another conversation was taking place in a neat house in Lindsey Row, facing the River Thames in Chelsea. It was the home of the upstart American born painter, James Whistler. The cantankerous Whistler had for a long time denied that he was born in Lowell, Massachusetts. The city blessed with hosting the auspicious occasion of his arrival in the world, he contended, was St Petersburg, Russia.

This morning, the dandyish Whistler sprawled in an armchair, stroking his ample moustache and glowering through his eyeglass at a younger man sitting opposite, filling the air with the scented fumes of a Turkish cigarette. He was just as dandyish as Whistler and, in a lapel, he wore the blood red ribbon of some decoration.

To the coterie who enjoyed justified reputations as the cream of London's artistic and literary talent, this man was nicknamed "Owl" but some other people in some other places knew him as "Mr. O".

'I'm not having it, Owl, my dear fellow,' Stated Whistler emphatically. 'Not having it at all. I suppose you have hawked it all around the daubers in London and they won't touch it. Now, you know I consider you to be a devil of a fellow. You're an adventurer who should be in top boots and a plumed hat. There's no man better as an artists' agent; nor can anyone equal you at discovering exquisite ceramics and the finest examples of antique furnishings but never have I known you to try to sell something sight unseen. You come here, with this yarn about a box containing a relic of American history of very high value but you haven't even brought it with you. How's a man to make a judgment when he hasn't seen the object on offer?'

'It's far too valuable to be treated lightly.' Owl said. 'One cannot just carry it from place to place as if it were some common object.'

Whistler gave a sharp laugh. 'I'll wager you tried this sight unseen dodge in the studios of all those who consider themselves to be the great men of English art. I suppose the Pre-Raphaelite bunch—Rossetti, Burne-Jones, Madox Brown and the rest—were all too busy living in the Middle Ages to notice the Nineteenth Century passing them by. So, under the mistaken notion that I am an American, you turn up here to try your luck with old Jimmy Whistler.'

'But you *are* an American, Jimmy,' objected Owl. 'It's widely known that you were born in Lowell and were once a cadet at West Point.'

'Bosh! I was born where I say I was born and St Petersburg is far more attractive than Lowell. Yes, I was a West Point cadet and when it was decided that the US Military Academy and I should part company, there was near hysterical joy on both sides. I have no special regard for the United States. Did I ever tell you my mother is descended from an old Southern family? And, anyway, who are you to question my word? You, who claim to be heir to various estates in Portugal and that you hold a royal honour of Portugal, the ribbon of which you are, even now, sporting in your coat, whether you have any right to or not. Let's not forget all the many stories from the time you were absent from London for so many years. You claim you were associated with the bomb-throwing Felice Orsini's attempt to kill the Emperor of the French and escaped while Orsini went under the guillotine. Then there are the yarns about your living as a card-sharper and diving for lost treasure in some ocean or other.'

'All true,' declared Owl, standing and striking a pose which he hoped looked heroic.

'Gammon!' replied the painter. 'I suspect you know the whole of London's artistic colony can see through your tall tales but nobody minds since you're an all-round good fellow and you have gifts peculiar to yourself.'

Whistler suddenly lowered his voice and said: 'I'll tell you the reason why I'm not in the market for this relic, pig in a poke, cat in a bag or whatever it is, Owl, my dear fellow.'

'What is it?'

'I'm broke.'

'Broke, Jimmy—you? But you're only just back from half a year in Chile.'

'Where I went to paint and for no other reason,' Whistler said firmly. 'The fact that I arrived there just as Chile and Spain went to war was a coincidence, so discount the silly rumour that I went as a spy for one government or the other. I put Jo in charge of my affairs while I was gone and I had hopes of her selling a set of etchings I had recently completed. There were no buyers which shocked me because, as you know, I'm considered a dab hand with an etching needle. I found Jo in low water financially when I returned and things are not much better now.'

Joanna Hiffernan, a copper haired Irish beauty, was Whistler's mistress and model and the subject of his painting *White Girl,* which caused a sensation when first exhibited.

Whistler suddenly adopted the tones of a street corner cadger: 'I don't suppose, old fellow, that you can find a pound or two to help a man out until I gather some tin by selling some work.'

'Sorry, Jimmy,' Owl answered quickly. 'I'm under the squeeze myself. As you know, I'm marrying Frances in the summer and hoping to buy a little place in Putney. You know how things are these days. Every penny has all but gone before a man earns it.'

There were no hard feelings between the pair because they could not help each other by handing over money, although Owl's chief concern was to get the box from Birkenhead off his hands since he believed there would be a fairly intensive search for it. He had never yet felt the hand of the law clamped on his shoulder and he had no desire to feel it at this stage of his life. He was approaching marriage to his statuesque and handsome cousin, Frances and, while there was no guarantee that holy matrimony would cure his criminal ways, it was likely to make him more cautious.

Owl stepped out of Whistler's house into the road on the other side of which flowed the River Thames. He paused for a minute or two to light a fresh cigarette and stood thinking about the box and how best he could secrete it in a safe place until the threat of police action blew over. He reflected on how he came to engineer the theft of the box the contents of which was unknown to him. He was simply told it was something of historic importance, particularly to Americans and it would gather value year by year. In the spirit of maintaining honour among thieves, he asked no questions. Among the lower echelons of criminality, where he was known as Mr. O, it was understood that he could acquire almost anything useful to breakers of the law.

At the more rarefied level of painters' studios and salons where the newest exquisite glass and china was collected and swooned over, he was known as a swashbuckler who could supply anything in the fine art line. No questions asked, of course.

He stood finishing his cigarette in his customary sucking and gulping fashion and he recalled how he was commissioned to lift the box from the Birkenhead villa. An eccentric American collector, living obscurely in London heard of the box, wanted it for his gallery of Americana and set certain wheels turning to give felonious employment to Mr. O, Sephton and Twist.

Then, for the first time in his adventuring in the murky world below the respectable surface of Queen Victoria's Britain, a deal turned sour on him. He had not counted on just how eccentric his eccentric client was. For, when it came to delivering the box to him, he found the man had taken a sudden notion to return to America and he did so, lock, stock and barrel, leaving no forwarding address. Not only was O unpaid for his risky activities in the north of England, he had on his hands the box containing he knew not what. Something else he did not know was that the man of distinction in Birkenhead, the victim of the theft, had no desire for the British authorities to know of the crime. He feared they might be justified in claiming the box as properly belonging to the United States. Consequently, there was no police investigation because the police never heard of the theft.

All O knew of the contents of the box was that it was chiefly of interest to Americans so he considered his best prospect as a buyer was James Whistler, the American he knew best, though Whistler persisted in sticking to the fantasy of his birth in St Petersburg. Rebuffed by Whistler, O was thrown into a quandary. He stood on the margin of the Thames, finishing his cigarette. As usual, he smoked it down to the merest scrap of a butt which he could scarcely hold in his fingers.

He tossed the butt away. Then he almost jumped in the air. It might have been the stimulation of his scented Turkish tobacco or the sharp wind blowing off the wide river, but something brought an almost miraculous inspiration to him. He suddenly knew where to deposit the burdensome box.

He tilted his tall hat to a rakish angle and, swinging his stick like a man conducting an invisible orchestra, strode jauntily off alongside the river, the most relieved man in London.

CHAPTER 3

THE MEN FROM GEORGIA

The streets of the dockland area of Liverpool were crowded and the throngs made up a mosaic of the people of the world. Seamen of every rank and nation rubbed shoulders with each other: the skinny young cabin boys; the smartly uniformed officers; the Chinese and Lascar deckhands and the tanned and bearded old salts who had spent their lives before the mast and had seen every wonder of the world.

There were voyagers of every class: the prosperous men of business just arrived in the country or just about to leave it, both of them travelling in the interests of profit and the families of emigrants, hopeful of new lives under new skies far away. There were beggars, one with a model of a battered ship on the crown of his hat, the mark of the sailor (supposedly) ruined by shipwreck. Ragged young women accompanied by two or three wan youngsters wandered among the crowd, telling sad tales of a seaman husband and father (supposedly) lost beneath the waves. Ladies of easy virtue prowled the scene with their eyes peeled for the black reinforced top hats of the policemen prominent above the two-way tide of bobbing heads. The harsh yells of hot pie vendors and newspaper sellers created a background anthem to the activity.

Through this swirling mass of bodies moved three men whose garb gave away their nationality as American. All three were tall and skinny, thin-faced and with hollow cheeks which suggested they had all endured periods of deprivation. They wore long black topcoats and black hats whose broad brims spoke of their New World origins. One had a limp which caused him to drag his toes along the ground.

It would strike any observer who was familiar with the details of the great war between the States, now nearly two years into history, that if this trio had served in it, they must have been with the defeated ill-fed and ill-equipped forces of the Southern Confederacy.

Such was indeed the case. Ex-Sergeant-Major Lewis Sadler; ex-Sergeant-Major Jefferson Dobbs and ex-Sergeant Ned Grandon were Georgians and a special breed of Georgian at that. They were "Georgia Crackers", men who claimed they could trace their ancestry back to the earliest settlers in the State—some of whom were British convicts—when it was a British province. They had a reputation as great boasters but not every Georgian was happy with the title of Cracker because, to some, it signified a poor white class. Sadler, Dobbs and Grandon took pride in it for their regiment, nicknamed "Vavasour's Georgia Crackers" distinguished itself trying to hold back the vastly superior force with which Union General William Tecumsah Sherman invaded Georgia, killing, burning and plundering. They were the only Georgia troops to stand up to Sherman; the others were withdrawn from facing his murderous progress but its commander defied military authority and, with inferior numbers, continued fighting.

This worked a reversal of fortune for the regiment. Hitherto and for most of the war, its commander, General Edmund Vavasour was known for his blunders and some had even handed him the dubious palm of the South's most incompetent soldier.

Post war, when he saw the tit-for-tat reprisals that the Reconstruction policies of Union President Andrew Johnson and his South-hating colleagues in the Radical wing of the Republican Party unleashed in Georgia, retired General Vavasour devised his own plan for the future of the State to which he had a fierce devotion. He also founded a movement to support and further his plan. This gathered strong support in Britain where Georgia had well-wishers as well as manufacturers and merchants who had been involved in the risky wartime business of seeking profits by sending precious cargoes into the Confederate States, hopefully eluding the blockade of the Southern coast by the US Navy.

In the great shadowy post-Civil War conflict in Georgia, anyone might be shot at any time, often with flimsy justification, so Vavasour kept his movement strictly secret. Some word of it leaked out and many old Confederates laughed and said it looked as if old Vavasour was setting up another blunder. Men of his old command, however, rallied to him. Where once they reviled him, they now honoured him for ridding the regiment of its blundering reputation and for earning glory with the heroic but futile resistance to Sherman's brutal invasion of their native State.

Sadler, Dobbs and Grandon were despatched to England to accomplish certain tasks for the General's movement. They were to meet their supporters in London to clarify for them the aims of the movement; to firm up its establishment in England and to organise a regular system of communication between the English group and the headquarters in Georgia. They were also to investigate the possibilities of the English group finding supporters further afield, in Wales, Scotland and Ireland.

Using the trans-Atlantic cable, General Vavasour had already placed a notice, in one of the leading London papers, warning of the forthcoming initial meeting. It was couched in prearranged code. Further meetings would be arranged by the three visitors.

There was one task which the General declared was first, foremost and paramount. While in Liverpool, the three were to cross the Mersey to the Birkenhead home of a distinguished American who would give them a large, firmly sealed box. They were not to open it nor to examine it but guard it with their lives and bring it to the General.

As they walked through the waterfront crowd, they had just left the ferry from Birkenhead. Sadler and Dobbs looked disgruntled and worried. Both were similar types: tough and uncompromising in their views, though Sadler had a measure of thoughtful discretion that fitted him for a leadership role. Dobbs had a more mercurial streak in him. He was a hardy Cracker, well suited to the battlefield. A resort to firearms seemed to him the swiftest way to settle a grave difference.

Ned Grandon seemed not particularly concerned that the trio had failed in the task on which the General laid most emphasis. In fact, his two companions noted that, as usual, there was a temperamental gulf between themselves and Grandon. His mind seemed always to be on something concerning himself and not on the mission in hand.

They had just suffered a severe blow that appeared to have blighted that mission from the very start. Arrived in England only the day before, they spent the night in a dockland hotel, in reality little more than a mariners' doss house and, the next morning, set out for Birkenhead and the box. They were ordered to take it with them to London, the next destination on their itinerary, then ultimately back to Georgia. However, their plans went badly awry when they met the distinguished exile at his Birkenhead home.

For he did not have the mysterious box. It was recently stolen in an audacious burglary.

The exile had no idea who had taken it and he stipulated that he must be obeyed. For his own good reasons, he did not want any word of the theft to leak out and reach the British authorities. The trio from Georgia now faced an acute dilemma; the box was stolen; they were required to go to London to further the General's plans and they had been given only a limited amount of money to cover their operations in England. The General had insisted that bringing the box to Georgia was a major objective of their expedition to Europe. But could they be diverted into a search for it, which could eat into their limited finances when other duties ordered by the General were pressing? Each man had an issue of money and there was a fund of ready finance for general use. It was agreed that if need be, each man would contribute whatever remained of his allowance to the general funds.

Lewis Sadler, being the senior of the two Sergeants-Major, was designated leader of the trio. Almost since the start of this venture, he had been quietly observing the demeanour of ex-Sergeant Ned Grandon. There was no doubt of Grandon's courage and devotion to duty during the war. In the regiment's attempt to hold back Sherman's savage progress through Georgia, he led his platoon by example. He took personal risks while, at the same time, he kept any hint of panic among the men dampened down and urged them to fight as an effective unit. Then, he was carried out of the thick of the action when a Yankee musket ball shattered his ankle, leaving him with a permanent limp.

Back home in post-war Georgia, he assisted the General in forming the defiant organisation which the controversial old warrior began to call "The League" and smacked of some old European brotherhood of patriots serving an heroic cause. He was, however, a changed man. Always with something on his mind, it seemed.

When it came to planning the expedition to Britain, Grandon positively pestered General Vavasour to be allowed to go with Sadler and Dobbs. The General felt the move called for only two men but allowed Grandon to go after he revealed something of his wandering life. As a boy, he had lived for time with a great uncle in London and still had a cousin there. Later, as a young seaman, he visited Liverpool several times and had some knowledge of the city.

As a travelling companion, Grandon proved less than desirable. Naturally morose, he seemed to become more so as their sea voyage proceeded. He was given to long spells of silence and hardly seemed at all interested in the business in hand. Even the news of the theft of the box failed to stir him where it brought forth colourful soldiers' expletives from Sadler and Dobbs. The latter had the urge to go forth and shoot someone, but he did not know who. Grandon was notably quiet and almost unconcerned. It was almost as if Ned Grandon was following his own strictly secret agenda.

Sadler was grateful that Jefferson Dobbs, for all his impetuous character, was a stolid Georgia Cracker, keeping his wits about him and ready for whatever came next in this mission which, with the loss of the Birkenhead box, looked to be unravelling at its very start.

The trio shoved their way through the dockland crowd, heading for their hotel-cum-dosshouse where they could talk their problems over. Sadler and Dobbs had a faint hope that they might discover the thieving hands into which the box had fallen and retrieve it. Grandon shrugged and said whatever they tried would be all right by him. The trouble with this move was that it would mean spending more time in Liverpool where, originally, they planned to leave for London the day after they collected the box from Birkenhead.

At heart, Sadler and Dobbs knew that their faint hope really amounted to no hope. They knew that Liverpool, like any large seaport, must have a widespread underworld of assorted villainy, dealing in every class of crime. They also knew that if the box was lost in such a sinister morass of lawlessness, it was likely to stay lost. With Ned Grandon contributing nothing to the decision, it was decided to stay one more day in Liverpool to try to locate the box. But, to themselves, Sadler and Dobbs admitted that the decision was chiefly a face-saving device for when they appeared before the General in Georgia minus the box. They wanted to be able to give him the impression that they had made a lengthy search for it before giving up hope and moving on to London.

Why the General set such store by the box and whatever it contained was a mystery to them but when he spoke of it, he seemed to think of it as a Holy Grail which would bestow some kind of blessing on what he called "the Objective" meaning the end his "League" was set up to achieve. Lewis Sadler was painfully aware that failure to secure the stolen object General Vavasour desired so earnestly might be an omen and the expedition to England was doomed to end as another Vavasour blunder.

The trio returned to their lodging where Sadler and Dobbs discussed their chances of finding the box. Both knew it was merely a token exercise because they did not have an inkling as to where they should even begin. Again, Ned Grandon took no part in the discussion. He sat to one side, looking morose as ever and when Sadler sneaked a glance he looked positively shifty.

The following morning brought a shock.

The trio's docklands resting place could justify its claim to be an hotel by having a set of cubby holes, not much better than cramped closets which were dignified by the name of "rooms" in which the guests slept. These imparted a measure of privacy.

Sailors' doss houses usually accommodated their guests in large dormitory type rooms. These offered no privacy and, at night, were rendered anything but restful with unmusical snoring and coughing, all under a low-hanging pall of harsh tobacco smoke.

The following morning, after a sleep troubled by anxious dreams, centred on the loss of the Birkenhead box, Lewis Sadler stepped out of his cubby hole of a "room" expecting to find at least one of his companions already up. The plan was that the three would go downstairs together to the canteen-like room where breakfast was served.

Sadler found he was the only one up but a couple of minutes later, Jefferson Dobbs came out of his cramped resting place, yawning. It looked as if Ned Grandon was oversleeping so Sadler and Dobbs looked into his "room" then recoiled and looked at each other in bewilderment.

Grandon and all his baggage were gone.

'Maybe he's forgotten we're staying an extra day and we're going tomorrow,' said Dobbs. 'Maybe he's packed his gear and taken it downstairs, ready to move off.'

Sadler remembered Grandon's demeanour ever since they took ship for Liverpool and his brooding attitude of recent days.

'No,' he said. 'I felt all along he was up to something—and now I know it.'

The two went downstairs where in the entrance hall, they found the proprietor of the establishment, a hefty, heavily bearded ex-mariner named Salty Sheldon, who looked as if he could give a good account of himself in a brawl in any waterfront dive from China to Peru. The air was thick with the odour of cooking issuing from the kitchen which Sheldon referred to as "the galley".

'Ah, gents, your mate left a short time ago. Said he was going on ahead of you.' He had a harsh, nasal Merseyside accent.

'He was up so early I thought he was out to shoot the moon—y'know, jump ship without paying his score—y'never know what some of the scallies that stay here will do next. But he was all right. Paid up right as rain when he'd had breakfast, picked up his cargo and shoved off.'

'Did he say where he was going?' asked Sadler.

Sheldon appeared slightly surprised.

'No, I figured you were all bound for the same place and he'd just gone ahead of you but he did ask if the London train still left from Lime Street Station. Seems he knows something about Liverpool. I told him I thought so but I know more about ships than trains.'

Dobbs looked at Sadler excitedly. 'Lime Street Station is not far,' he said. 'It's just a short distance down Paradise Street. If we hurry, we might catch him before he gets on a train.'

Salty Sheldon moved quickly, putting his bulk between Dobbs and the street door. His pugnacious face was frowning and his hands were balled into outsize fists.

'Not so fast,' he growled. 'I was too long before the mast to fall for this kind of Swell Mob dodge. You get your mate to leave all proper, then you make out he's jumped ship and chase after him, leaving payment for your beds and breakfasts behind you. And I never see you again. Oh, sure, you've left your gear here but the whole cargo'll turn out to be not worth a bean. Smart Alecky Yankee tricks won't wash with me.'

'Don't call us Yankees', hooted Dobbs angrily.

'That's not our game', said Sadler. 'We can't go outdoors as we are. It's too cold and our topcoats are upstairs. We'll get them and we'll pay you before we go out.'

He and Dobbs clattered up the uncovered wooden stairs, weaving their way between half a dozen newly awake fellow lodgers going down for breakfast. They came down again in their topcoats and hats and Sadler had a fistful of golden coins. Salty Sheldon was standing at the foot of the stairs. Sadler thrust the coins into his hand.

'That's probably more than we owe you but you can give us the change when we come back—and we *will* come back!' he said, glowering at Sheldon.

Salty Sheldon looked mollified and, as the two rushed down the hall towards the street door, he called: 'Listen, gents, I didn't mean to—'

But Sadler and Dobbs, moving at top speed, were already out of the front door and running for Paradise Street. When they reached that link with the noisy and colourful world of the docklands it was busy with early morning traffic. Dockers, brawny and skinny, hastened towards the crowded masts of vessels being loaded or unloaded and bespectacled clerks from shipping offices hastened toward their desks. Heavily laden wagons, drawn by plodding, big-boned horses, conveyed cargoes of infinite variety bound for every quarter of the globe.

Sadler and Dobbs ran against this moving stream of humanity, animals and vehicles, dodging pedestrians and sometimes shoving them aside to make speedy progress which was accepted behaviour on a crowded Victorian street. All the time, they kept their eyes skinned for Ned Grandon's characteristic, toe-dragging limp, but did not see it. Possibly, he had a greater start on them than they realised.

They left Paradise Street behind and were in Lime Street with the bulk of railway station's building, modelled on a French chateau, in front of them. Lime Street, was one of Liverpool's busiest thoroughfares and the two Georgians were panting and slowing in pace as they neared the station. They had few kindly thoughts for Salty Sheldon who had delayed their start with his quibbling and probably caused Grandon to gain the advantage over them.

By the time they reached the long flight of stone steps leading up to the entrance to the station, both felt almost unable to continue running. Panting heavily and on leaden legs, they mounted the steps slowly. The great cavern of the station was noisy with hissing steam, the clanging and shunting of rolling stock and the hubbub of a mass of passengers moving in every direction. The pair threaded their way through the travellers with their eyes skinned but there was no sign of Ned Grandon among them.

'Where does the London train go from?' shouted Dobbs to the first porter he saw.

'Platform Seven, up yonder, Skipper,' answered the man.

They hurried to that platform and found its entrance barrier guarded by the customary ticket-collector. There was no train standing at the platform but in the far distance one was heading out of the gloom of the station into the wintery sunshine.

Sadler asked about the London train and the ticket-collector jerked his thumb at the one dwindling in the distance, leaving rags of smoke straggling behind it.

'That's her', said the man. 'You missed her by a minute and a half, lad.'

'Did you see a man with a lame foot get aboard her?' asked Sadler.

'Yes, he was almost the last man aboard.'

Sadler grunted and Dobbs growled in frustration, each thinking how they might have caught up with Grandon but for Salty Sheldon delaying the start of their pursuit.

'We have a regular talent for losing things,' Dobbs said. 'First the box in Birkenhead yesterday and Grandon here today. I'd give my eye teeth to know what game he's playing. He was a sure enough damned cuss to get along with but I never figured on him running out on us that way.'

'Nor I,' Sadler said. 'I watched him for some time. He seemed to support the General and his objective all the way but I couldn't help feeling his mind was on something else all the time. When we nail him in London—and, by thunder, I'm determined that we *shall*—we'll get to the bottom of his antics. He has a heap of money with him that really belongs to our common pot.'

There was no question of leaving for London that same day for the next train, leaving in the late afternoon, would arrive in the capital after dark and that would lead to complications in finding their accommodation. The General had made arrangements for all three of his agents to stay with one of the League's

British supporters, a maker of breech-loading rifles in Camden Town. Like many of the British supporters, he had supplied the struggling forces of Dixie during the Civil War with armaments through blockade-breaking.

Neither man had ever been to England before and both had the uneasy feeling that looking for Grandon in a city so big as they understood the British capital to be would be seeking a needle in a haystack. Neither communicated his qualms to the other.

Totally disgruntled through meeting frustration every time they turned a corner in Liverpool, they trudged back to Paradise Street, heading for Salty Sheldon's establishment. The atmosphere had turned several degrees colder and the sky darkened. Sadler and Dobbs shuddered and, just as they were passing an eating house at the corner of Paradise Street, the drifting aroma of cooking reminded Jefferson Dobbs that the morning's alarms at Salty Sheldon's hotel had robbed them of breakfast.

The aroma was powerful enough to turn their steps towards the door of the establishment. They found it catered to the appetites of mariners. Its décor must not have changed in over fifty years. The ceiling was low; there were models of old sailing vessels on a shelf running the length of one wall and a faded engraving of Lord Nelson was on the wall behind the long counter with sections of sea charts as neighbours. A set of oaken booths, offering privacy to customers, was established along the walls.

At this hour of the morning, the place was empty save for a little man in a too-long waiter's apron, leaning against the counter, apparently asleep. He jerked into wakefulness when the two Georgians entered.

'I'll take your order at the counter, lads. Then you take a seat,' he said in the nasal tones of Merseyside to which the pair were becoming accustomed. His demeanour suggested that the ethos of the house was akin to that aboard a merchantman. The menu was based solidly on meat and vegetables, geared to appetites sharpened by sea breezes and Sadler and Dobbs found there was plenty of it. And it was highly satisfactory.

Seated in one of the booths with a table between them, they had been eating for only a few minutes when a couple of men entered. Such was the position of the booth occupied by the Georgians in relation to the door and the counter that they could not see the newcomers but they heard them negotiate with the waiter. Then the newly arrived pair tramped across the floor and settled in the booth next to their own. The little waiter delivered their orders a short time later.

The tops of the booths were open and gruff conversation floated over the dividing partition into Sadler and Dobbs' booth. It was of a nondescript nature and of no interest to the Georgians until the gruffer of the two voices said:

'I heard Bill Twist was talkin' too much in the Mermaid and Flagon the other night. Almost went too far but his mate, Sephton, shut him up.'

The second man gave a harsh laugh. 'I'm not surprised, Bill never could keep his lip buttoned up when he's full of grog. The scuppers have never nabbed 'em yet, but Bill's gab'll put both of 'em in shackles one day.'

'Yeh, nothing so sure,' said the other. 'It seems Bill was boasting about a big job they did at some toff's place over the water and got away with something special.'

Lewis Sadler's hand, holding a fork conveying a piece of beef to his mouth, stilled in mid-air while Jefferson Dobbs almost choked on a portion of potato. They had both been in Liverpool long enough to know that 'over the water' referred to the opposite shore of the River Mersey, the Cheshire shore, where Birkenhead was located.

Sadler rose to his feet, put a finger to his mouth to signal silence then moved forward, beckoning to Dobbs to follow him. They slipped out of the booth quickly and made a noiseless and speedy invasion of the next one.

Frozen in surprise and staring at them from either side of a table bearing their meals were a couple of men, one large and the other smaller, wearing labourers' clothing. Each bore a strong resemblance to the ruffians shown in the 'Known to the Police' engravings in the crime pages of the newspapers.

Before he knew it, the larger of the two found one of the pair of lean apparitions in black topcoats sitting on the seat beside him. The second was standing menacingly over his companion with his hand in his coat pocket suggestive of his levelling a hidden gun.

'Wh-what's this?' stammered the larger. 'Are you scuppers, or what?'

'Not scuppers,' said Sadler, beside him. 'We're a damned sight worse than scuppers. We're not telling you who we are but we'll tickle you're innards with hot lead if you play smart with us.'

Sadler had his hand in the coat pocket close to the man beside him, the larger of the two and the man felt something hard prod him in the ribs.

'It's a Colt revolver, Cousin, and if you don't believe me, just you get my dander up and I'll let daylight into you. We want to know about the two gents you mentioned awhile back—the pair who robbed a house in Birkenhead.'

'Don't know much. I only heard rumours about them,' said the man. He was obviously scared but he was trying to hold on to any information he had.

He received another prod in the ribs, more severe than the last.

'You know plenty, Cousin' growled Sadler. 'Their names, for instance. C'mon, their names, before my friend yonder and I get tired of fooling around and start shooting.'

'Charlie Sephton and Bill Twist,' said the man, now shaking with fear.

'And this place where they hang out. Sounds like a saloon or a pub. Where is it?'

'The Mermaid and Flagon? It's in Hackin's Court, near Cape Town Dock.'

'And are they in there every night?'

'Near enough every night. They're demons for their grog.'

'Are they likely to be there tonight, Cousin?'

'I reckon so.'

'Well, my friend yonder and I will be there to have a chat with them so, if you should meet them in the course of the day and mention that we're coming calling and you scare them away from taking what's coming to them, by thunder, we'll come after you. What do they call you, Cousin?'

'Dick Rimmer.'

'And your dithering friend back there?'

'Jackie Fullbrook,' answered the second man for himself though he was still intimidated by scowling Jefferson Dobbs pointing the weapon inside his pocket.

'And what do this Sephton and Twist look like? Sadler asked. 'We wouldn't want to pump lead into the wrong gents.'

'Both small. Sephton has a scrubby black beard and Twist stoops and has a scrap of hair at the front of his chin—just a patch of it—like Frenchmen have. And both of 'em wear working men's moleskin caps.'

Dick Rimmer seemed eager to gush forth information now that he had started.

'One last thing. Do these two gentlemen carry firearms?' asked Sadler.

This touched a patriotic spark in Rimmer. 'Certainly not! They might be scallies but they're Englishmen. Pistols and knives are for foreigners,' he said heatedly.

Sadler chuckled. 'Grubby foreigners, like my friend and I, who don't play according to the rules of cricket, eh? Well, just remember, we'll be lurking around, ready to deal out retribution with our pistols if you say you've seen us or if you say anything about how we aim to visit the Mermaid and Flagon. Get on with your eating if you have the stomach for it.'

The two Georgians made a quick exit and returned to their interrupted meals in the next door booth.

'They're just a pair of waterfront no-accounts,' murmured Sadler.

'Sure, but mighty useful in leading us to the pair who stole the box,' said Dobbs.

'Unless they led us up the garden path.'

After the disappointments of the day, Sadler was not ready to accept that, at last, they had been dealt a stroke of luck.

In view of their need to take the train to London the following day, they knew the next step in their quest for the box must be taken at once.

Back at their accommodation, Salty Sheldon frowned when they inquired as to the location of Hackin's Court and the Mermaid and Flagon.

'You'd best not drop anchor in those waters for too long,' he said. 'There's some uncommon dangerous fish in 'em.' After their delaying misunderstanding that morning which almost certainly contributed to their loss of Ned Grandon, Sheldon was very much chastened. He drew a sketch map indicating where the court and the pub could be found.

The first shades of evening were falling when Sadler and Dobbs set out to walk to Hackin's Court, deep in dockland, where a forest of tall masts and furled sails rose starkly against a darkening sky. Full night was almost blanketing the region by the time they found Hackin's Court, a cramped cul-de-sac squeezed between a row of ill-kept houses. Tenement-like dwellings huddled along either side of the court and the dim illumination of lamp and candle from their grimy windows mottled the cobbled footway.

At the blind end of the cul-de-sac crouched a small tavern, making its presence felt by extra bright lights and the bellowing by many voices of a sad ballad, long woven into the fabric of Liverpool, the tale of Maggie May, a 'Judy' (girl) who was no better than she ought to be.

> 'Oh, Maggie, Maggie May
> 'They have taken you away
> 'And you'll never walk down Lime Street anymore...'

Evidently, this was the Mermaid and Flagon and the grog was flowing good and strong there.

Sadler and Dobbs walked up to the building above the door of which swung an old painted sign showing a fish-tailed woman with a truly evil leer, holding an outsize flagon. They opened the door which immediately caused an almost tangible gust of warm air, alcoholic fumes, tobacco smoke, bodily odours to gush out. Riding on it was a raucous snatch of song:

'Oh, I was a bloody fool,
'In the port of Liverpool,
'The first time that l came home from sea...'

The interior was crowded with the motley mixture of humanity to be expected in the dock quarter of a major port. Deck officers and deckhands, juvenile cabin boys, various grades of "greasers" from steam vessels that were increasing in number, every type of dockside cargo handler and a scattering of painted ladies were all imbibing strong drink and voicing alcohol-induced song.

Some were seated at tables and others stood around in knots and clusters, swinging pint pots and bellowing the song.

The two Georgians' eyes had to pierce a veil of tobacco smoke to distinguish faces, even those of individuals quite close to them and Dobbs suddenly nudged Sadler.

'Look. Over to the left—two moleskin caps,' he said. The wearers of the caps were two undersized men created by slum conditions and poor diets to be burglars or what the underworld called "snakesmen", thin enough to slither through any narrow window or tight aperture, As they stared at the pair, one man turned his head and showed a dark patch of hair under his mouth, a not notably successful attempt to cultivate a French imperial beard.

Lewis Sadler grinned. 'Look at the size of them. We could each pick one of them up from the back and rush out of the door. It's on a swivel hinge, so we'll have no trouble with locks. And they'll be out in picturesque Hackin's Court before they know it.'

Dobbs grinned back at Sadler. The idea suited him because he relished a little rough handed action now and again. Both moved cautiously behind Sephton and Twist unnoticed by their neighbours who were intent on drinking and murdering the song.

As if acting on a word of command, the Georgians sprang forward, each encircled the waist of a burglar with his arms, hoisted him off his feet, whirled him around, causing two ale pots to fly in the air and neighbouring drinkers to be splashed with grog. Sadler and Dobbs turned and ran for the door, each with his bewildered burden. Sephton and Twist were shaken out of their State of stunned surprise the moment they were carried out into the cold night air and both began to struggle but to no avail.

Both were slammed up against a grimy brick wall in a dark corner across the court from the pub. If the nature of their snatching caused any concern among their fellow imbibers it was not demonstrated. No one followed the captors and captives out of the pub. This was because it was not unknown for patrons of the Mermaid and Flagon to be suddenly seized by men who made an abrupt appearance. In those cases, the men were officers of Liverpool Police, not men of American appearance in dark clothing and broad-brimmed hats. Whoever did such snatching, their fellow patrons found it best to mind their own business and say nothing.

Sephton and Twist, pinned against the wall, felt the grog that was so comforting so short a time ago, turn sour inside them when the dim light showed that each of their captors was flourishing a large pistol. Having at last caught up with the pair who stole the Birkenhead box, Sadler and Dobbs were less cautious about showing their Colt revolvers in this country where firearms were not so universally accepted as in the New World.

Lewis Sadler had his left hand on Charlie Sephton's chest, pinning him against the wall. His other hand gripped his revolver the business end of which was almost touching the point of Sephton's nose.

'You took a box from a house in Birkenhead—where is it?' demanded Sadler.

Sephton opened and closed his mouth three or four times without managing to produce any words. All his attention was given to squinting at the barrel of the revolver almost tickling his nose. Next to him, Bill Twist made an attempt to wriggle free of Dobbs' grasp but, for all his lean frame, the Georgian proved remarkably powerful, shoving him back against the wall and prodding him in the region of the navel with his firearm.

'Your mate's lost the power of speech, bub, so let's hear the answer from you and if the cat's got your tongue, too, I'll give you a belly button to match the one nature gave you. C'mon, cough up—where is that box?'

'Dunno, mister, and that's God's honest truth.' Twist was sweating profusely and his voice was quivering with fear.

'All we know is it's somewhere in London. Mr. O took it there.'

'Who's Mr. O?' said Sadler and Dobbs in unison.

'The fella from London who put up the job,' said Sephton, finding a rather jittery voice at last. 'We don't know nothing about him. He just turned up at this pub and offered us the job. He's a real toff. Smokes Turkish cigarettes. Smokes 'em all the time, as if he's eatin 'em. Smokes 'em right down to nothing.'

'And he's a Dago,' put in Twist.

'A Dago?' queried Sadler.

'Yeh. From wherever Dagoes come from. He's all London style airs and graces but he's not a proper Englishman.'

'If he's not an Englishman, do you mean he might have taken the box to another country? Or does he live in London and is he holed up there with the box? And what's the whole story behind its theft, anyway? Do you know what's in that box?'

'No, I don't. I never ask questions when I'm asked to do a job. I just do the job.'

Sadler snorted in disgust. Now that Dobbs and he had their hands on the burglars it looked as if the pair could part with little genuine information simply because they did not have it. He was frustrated with the negative responses to his questions and, from what he could hear of it, Dobbs' interrogation of Twist, next to him, was meeting with no greater success. It seemed there were deeper implications to the theft of the box than appeared at first sight.

Elements of the affair marched through his mind as he continued to prod Sephton's undernourished body with the mouth of his revolver. The General, back in Georgia, wanted the box for some reason connected with his "League". The mysterious Mr. O, from London, wanted it so badly that he travelled north, found a couple of professional thieves and paid them to steal it. And nobody wanted the box more urgently than Lewis Sadler and Jefferson Dobbs.

So far as it could be tracked from the testimony of the burglars it was now in London, taken there by the 'Dago', Mr. O. Unless, of course, Mr. O, being a foreigner, had since spirited it out of the country. Further questioning brought forth nothing more valuable than two nuggets of information: the existence of Mr. O and the fact that he had taken the box to London.

Lewis Sadler indicated that Dobbs should relax his armed vigilance over Bill Twist and he took his own pistol away from Sephton's midriff. He jerked his head towards the glittering door of the Mermaid and Flagon.

'Scoot back to your grog,' he said.

Both of the miscreants looked at him dumbly then Sephton said: 'You mean you ain't going to hand us over to the scuppers for crackin' that crib over the water?'

'Cousin, we don't have time for that,' said Sadler. 'And I always believed our hometown preacher when he said our sins will surely find us out, so I reckon you two'll naturally fall into the hands of the scuppers all in good time. Meantime, we have other fish to fry.'

When he and Dobbs considered the fish they had to fry, they were alarmed at how much they must accomplish in a short space of time. They had to take the train for London the following morning. In London, they had to make contact with English members of the General's League who would settle them into accommodation and advise them of the time and place of the meeting between the visitors and British members of the league. This would have already been arranged by the British end of the venture and the advertisement "copy" already supplied to the press.

General Vavasour had stipulated that this meeting should be held as soon as possible after his representatives reached

London. He wanted every minute of their time in London taken up with the work of promoting the league and organising its tasks for the future.

Consulting the written schedule supplied by the general, they saw they were faced with an almost insurmountable set of duties. Furthermore, overshadowing all else, were the weighty burdens laid on their backs by occurrences after their arrival in England that were still unknown to the old warrior back in Georgia.

They had to somehow find the unknown Mr. O, make every effort to recover the box then track down Ned Grandon and find out why he deserted his travelling companions, apparently to pursue some affair of his own.

CHAPTER 4

DISRUPTION ON THE HOO

One thing Septimus Dacers found irksome in the unorthodox life he had chosen was the associated paperwork. If there was a private inquiry agent in London who could afford a secretary or even an office boy, Dacers had never heard of him. As a "one-man band", he had to attend to his accounts and correspondence himself. None of it was particularly difficult or time consuming but Dacers had an active itch that made him want to be on the move rather than sitting at his desk, writing. One of his chores in the one-man band was the mailing of his own letters.

This he quite enjoyed and he tried to accomplish it as early in the morning as he could, even before breakfast, It entailed walking along one side of the square to the busy road at the further end where there were shops and a pillar box, one of the stylish public postal boxes designed by Mr. Anthony Trollope, the novelist and Postal officer.

As ardent a Londoner as Dr Johnson, he always found the streets fascinating as they came to vigorous life soon after dawn. The workers of both sexes and every age, shape and size, filled the square and surrounding streets, rushing to earn their daily bread. Dacers was grateful that the world of commerce did not claim him as a youth and shackle him to a tall counting house stool for a life of drudgery, such as was endured by so many of these earnestly hurrying people.

His own immediate streets had not reached their full weight of pedestrian traffic as, carrying his few letters to be mailed, he turned out of his square and into the broader neighbouring street. He almost walked into a horse and rider standing still in the gutter. The horseman was tall and rangy with a thin face, hollow cheeks and eyes with an intense glow that warned Dacers of trouble.

He was dressed in the style of an English country gentleman with a billycock hat, a Norfolk jacket and riding breeches and boots. The lower half of his face was covered with a thick, pointed black beard.

Dacers, as a Victorian detective, working in a bearded age, had worn false whiskers in his time and he noted certain signs, including a whiff of the pungent gum that secured the beard, all showing it to be false. Curiously, the rider held his right arm behind his back.

As Dacers drew a little closer to him, the horseman leaned forward and his face came near enough for Dacers to notice a large wart over his left eyebrow.

'Are you Dacers?' he asked.

'I am,' said Dacers.

At once, the rider swung his arm from behind his back and the bright sunshine of the winter morning glinted off a long-barrelled revolver in his hand.

He aimed it directly at Dacers who, instinctively ducked down and, in desperation, lunged out with both fists, smiting the horse in the ribs with some force, causing it to snort and rear its forelegs in the air at the very moment the rider fired. The weapon had been aimed point blank at Dacers but, with the pistol jerked off target, the bullet went spinning into the air.

At the report, the horse plunged around nervously while the rider, holding his smoking gun, tried to control it with one hand. Then, a violent jerk from the animal unhorsed the rider and he was sent sprawling on the cobbles.

Dacers, doubled up in the gutter, watched him scramble around then he became aware that a commotion had arisen along the street some distance behind the rider, Women screamed and several male voices shouted panicky warnings.

'Hey! Clear the street!'

'Watch out yonder!'

'Get that horse out of the way!'

Down the street, coming at gathering speed was one of the worst hazards of early morning in the streets of London: a cattle stampede. In many respects, the city still had a rural face and what would become inner suburbs were still villages or small towns with farms surrounding them. Every day, cattle and flocks of sheep were driven into central London to Smithfield and other markets. Quite frequently, there would be an entanglement of vehicles and animals on a principal street, causing exchanges of blistering language between carters, cabbies and drovers and frantic attempts to restore order by frustrated policemen.

Worst of all was a stampede when some sudden noise frightened a herd of cattle or a flock of sheep. The creatures, already unnerved by being in the unfamiliar confines of a city, would run wild, mounting the pavements and knocking pedestrians over. Sheep were given to running in aimless, swirling circles all over the roadways and pavements.

There was a full scale stampede building up down the road, beyond the point where the horseman had tried to shoot Dacers. Possibly panic caused by the report of the pistol sent the animals charging onward, towards the corner where the rider was trying to control his mount, Dacers was attempting to scoot back into the square where he resided to escape the hooves of the cattle, now spread out from pavement to pavement. At any second, one or more police officers would appear on the scene, a point clearly realised by the downed horseman now scrambling to his feet. He still had his weapon in his hand but he had no time to risk another shot at Dacers before the frenzied beasts were upon him.

He came fully to his feet and, for an instant, stood as if paralysed full in the face of the charging creatures, staring at them as though hypnotised by them. Then he came to life and ran for the side of the street opposite Dacers. He progressed speedily though Dacers noticed that he had a lame foot which caused him to trail the toe of his boot along the ground with every step.

Dacers, shaken and bewildered crouched in the gutter, still holding his unmailed letters. He suddenly saw red. A surge of uncontrollable fury came over him. He wanted to cross the street and get his hands on the man who had almost put a bullet into him. He crammed the letters into the pocket of his top-coat as he came to his feet and, paying no heed to the mass of animals now almost level with him, he ran across the face of the torrent of drumming hooves, rolling eyes and snorting nostrils.

Mid-way across the road, he came to his senses and, with his heart in his mouth, realised the lunacy of charging directly under the noses of the frenzied creatures. Within the merest fragment of time, he would be pounded under their hooves. If he did not summon every breath in his lungs and pump his legs like pistons, he would never reach the opposite pavement which swam in his vision, seeming to be so far away as to be totally unattainable.

Then, he was suddenly there and striving to jump on to the opposing kerb at which point he came into contact with the far fringe of the stampede.

A panic stricken cow struck his side and sent him cannoning over the kerb and, going almost head over heels, he landed in a gasping heap on the far pavement.

With the breath knocked out of his lungs, he lay spreadeagled on the paving, acutely aware of the roiling sea of animal flesh and horns charging along only inches from his head. Summoning all his strength, he rolled close to the buildings on the inner side of the pavement and managed to sit up. He looked around for some sign of the limping horseman, but could not see him. He must been nearly as shaken as Dacers because of his own encounter with the runaway beasts but, in spite of his lame foot, he must have made off into the tangle of smaller streets lying beyond this side of the major street. There was a positive warren of them with associated alleyways and even a man with impaired movement would have no trouble in scooting into them and quickly getting out of sight.

Snorting with disgust, Dacers found his feet, leaned against a wall and watched the last of the runaway beasts go past him, followed by a squad of running drovers, waving their sticks and bellowing hoarsely. The stampede seemed not to have attracted the attention of any constables for which Dacers was grateful. He did not want to face the ponderous questioning of the average beat peeler as to why he should be targeted by the rider whose shot sparked off the charge of the market-bound animals. If the police were to be brought into it, he'd attend to it in his own way in consultation with his trusted friend, Inspector Amos Twells, of Scotland Yard.

As his nerves settled and his breathing became normal, he thought of venturing into the neighbouring side streets to search for the gunman but then he realised the limping man had too good a start on him and, by now, would have faded into obscurity. He thought of the man's horse which, animal like, had probably caught the panic of the cattle and was swept into the stampede. If it was found, its trappings might reveal something of the rider's identity but the efficiency of the man's attempt at murder suggested that he would have taken precautions against that.

Even as he thought of the shot that was fired at him, Dacers' eye fell on an object lying on the pavement. It was the long-barrelled pistol which the would-be assassin had obviously dropped in his scramble to escape the charging animals. Picking it up quickly, he thought that if the attempt on his life did come under police scrutiny, the pistol could be an invaluable clue.

The weapon was handsomely designed and, on a length of metal under the long barrel were the moulded letters: *"Remington New Model Army Pattern 1858"*. Then, on one of the hardwood facings of the butt, he found a set of faintly scratched letters. Most were difficult to read. A top line was totally undecipherable but it could have been a name. Below it was a worn scratch which had probably been a numeral and this was followed by blurred scratches decipherable as: *"Georgia Volunteer Infantry."*

So, once again, echoes of a faraway conflict that ended two years before were sounding in Dacers' life.

The blood-curdling incident of the murderous rider who seemed to be an orthodox English type from his billycock hat to his spurs had set his morning awry. He had never seen the man before although there was something about him that struck a chord of familiarity. Then he recalled that the man's voice momentarily carried him back to his tangles with the confidence tricksters known as the Dixie Ghosts; it also reminded him of Roberta Van Trask whose accent bore witness to her time spent in Washington, so close to Virginia. For all his style as an English country gentleman, the fellow's speech betrayed his origins. They were plainly in the Southern States of America.

Dacers felt like a man tied up by knotty problems and when he tried to unfasten some of the knots, he constantly discovered that he was entangled in something to do with the tragedy of the American Civil War. Somebody wanted him dead—but who? It was clearly somebody connected with the Southern States. Of anyone from that region who had cause to want his assassination, the Dixie Ghosts, whose criminal schemes he had a major hand in wrecking, had the most obvious grudge—but they were all in prison. Perhaps there were more involved in it than the handful who came to England, although they were certainly leaders in the great swindle and the crafty little man who went by the name of Fortune was certainly its originator.

The curious newspaper announcement which brought echoes of the Dixie Ghosts came to mind although there was nothing in it to suggest a direct link between the advertisers and the Dixie Ghosts. Nevertheless, it was odd that the mounted gunman, almost certainly from the Ghosts, should arrive just as the announcement showed up in the press.

It was plain that the attempt on his life was well planned. Dacers realised that his address and habits must have been watched for some time. The bearded, armed horseman must have monitored his morning trips to the post box, probably from some distance along the street, to know where to place himself to ambush Dacers at the precise point at which he crossed the road every morning.

Then there was the timing and style of his murder attempt. It was early morning on a crowded street where a shot was bound to be heard. Whoever fired it was sure to be noticed and his beard would be remembered. Very likely the horseman placed much confidence in both the beard and his smart countryman's outfit. If he left Dacers a corpse in the gutter and made a speedy getaway to some readily prepared refuge, quickly changed his clothing and got rid of the beard he could appear as a working man, a clerk or anybody but the stylish, bearded rider who killed a man in a street crowded with witnesses.

The audacious murder attempt was obviously coolly worked out. The man's costume and style gave him a certain persona that he could shed like an actor stripping off the trappings of a part. So long as he remained in his saddle, his most noticeable characteristic, his toe-dragging limp, remained hidden. However, that subterfuge was blown when the stampeding chaos he caused by his shot unhorsed him.

The Remington pistol, an American weapon, which had once been owned by someone in a Georgia regiment in the Civil War—possibly the gunman himself—heightened the emphasis of the Southern States in the riddle.

Dacers could not shake off the feeling that the announcement in the newspaper was of some significance in the attack on his life and every throw of the dice brought up the Dixie Ghosts.

The chilling indications were that the Dixie Ghosts were not done for, were hunting vengeance—and Septimus Dacers was in their sights.

CHAPTER 5

MISS VAN TRASK SHOWS HER METTLE

Richard, Theodore Van Trask's coachman, a large man who had once been a soldier, had a deft touch with the reins and he brought the family's open brougham into the square, halted it outside Mrs. Slingsby's address where he vacated his seat, stepped back to the door of the passenger compartment. He dutifully handed down Miss Roberta Van Trask, who was without her usual chaperone, Esther, and appeared to be as brisk and bright as the morning itself. She carried a large bag of raffia work.

Richard accompanied her up the steps to the door of the house and yanked the bell-pull then stood back with soldierly dignity until the door was opened by Emma, the maidservant.

'Miss Van Trask, calling on Mr. Dacers,' he announced.

Emma curtsied to Roberta. 'Good morning, mum. Please come in,' she said. After the visitor had entered and as she was closing the door, Emma said to Richard: 'Coachman, please take your coach around to the mews and wait.' She raised a hand to her lips and mimed someone drinking from a cup, conveying the message that he would receive some refreshment while waiting in the mews, the stable area at the rear of the house.

'Thank you, Mary,' he said, employing the name commonly used when addressing strange maidservants. Then he winked, betraying the waggish nature cloaked by his large frame and martial demeanour. Such exchanges were all part of the secret social lives lived by servants.

Mrs. Slingsby came bustling out of the innards of the house, beamed at Roberta and thought there must be a strengthening of affection between the two when Miss Van Trask was calling on Septimus Dacers so early in the morning without the usual formality of prior notice.

'Good morning, Miss Van Trask, you are very welcome,' she said, with a curtsey.

'Good morning, Mrs. Slingsby, Please excuse my lack of courtesy in calling without sending a prior card,' said the visitor.

'Don't mention it. If I may say so, you brighten this drab old house every time you call.' It was an apt comment for the American girl was looking particularly bright-eyed and was certainly elated, 'Please take a seat in the reception room while Emma brings Mr. Dacers from upstairs.'

Dacers found Roberta settled in the little reception room with the bag on her lap and was immediately aware of her high spirits. She looked as if she was concealing a great secret and could not wait to blurt it out.

This was the morning after his encounter with the bearded gunman and he was concealing his own great secret. He had not told Mrs. Slingsby or Emma how the mounted man lay in wait for him for fear that they might be frightened of his returning to the vicinity of the house and putting them in danger.

When he first met Theodore Van Trask to accompany him to Liverpool as bodyguard while investigating the secret building of Confederate ships for the war then raging, the US Embassy insisted that he carry a revolver, though British inquiry agents usually scorned firearms. When that assignment was ended, the Americans presented Dacers with the pistol and a small quantity of ammunition as souvenirs. On the night after the attempt on his life, he slept with the loaded weapon under his pillow and he resolved to go about his daily business armed since his life was no longer safe on the streets.

This morning, sight of Roberta drove considerations such as assassination on the street from his mind.

'Miss Van Trask, it is a joy to see you and in the very best of humours, too,' he greeted. 'I perceive the signs of spring are having a marked effect on you.'

'Indeed they are and they are making me bold enough to claim that at least one member of the female gender—namely myself—can demonstrate her fitness to be a detective.'

Dacers chuckled, remembering the morning a few days before when she effectively defeated him on that subject.

Then, from her raffia bag, she drew a folded page taken from a newspaper. She handed it to him and he saw that it was the page from the issue of a few days before carrying the notice addressed to someone, or perhaps a body of people, under the initials, LUB. Sight of it brought back the feeling he had when he first spotted it—that it was somehow connected with the case of the Dixie Ghosts. Since then he had totally forgotten about the announcement until it returned to mind after the encounter with the mounted gunman.

'Did you see this when it was new?' she asked.

'Yes and it intrigued me for a time. It brought back memories of the Dixie Ghosts but I can't say why. I eventually forgot all about it, though I recall there was mention of another message to follow.

'Yes and I have it here. From this morning's paper.'

'Which I haven't yet seen.'

She handed him the second communication, placed in the paper by one of Vavasour's London contacts on the General's instructions.

He read it quickly and gave a short laugh.

'Aha! The first one baffled me completely, except for a modicum of plain English, This second one is rather easier and I believe I have solved it without much trouble.'

'Mr. Dacers, the first of those messages puzzled me for days,' she said. 'I just knew there was something about it—something American—that was shouting out to me but I just could not understand it. Now you say you have solved the second part. Please, you must tell me what it means.'

He smiled, shook his head and said somewhat teasingly. 'Oh, no. You claim to have solved the first part so let's start with that so we have a full picture.'

'Very well. Take the first part: *The good father is wrong.* Have you ever heard of Father Abram Joseph Ryan?'

'No.'

'Neither had I until very recently when I read about him in one of the literary journals Father receives from home. They are beginning to call him the Poet Laureate of the Confederacy. He is a Catholic priest, a son of Irish immigrants born in the South and devoted to Dixie. He joined the Confederate Army as a chaplain and distinguished himself on the battlefield, giving the last rites to dying men and carrying the wounded to places of safety. With the collapse of the South, he wrote a poem, *The Conquered Banner,* which is popular with both sides. It makes a plea for the South to accept the furling of its flag but to always remember the thousands of brave and devoted men—of whom his brother was one—and women who died in its service.'

Roberta paused and, for a moment, her face clouded and she said: 'That's a sentiment thousands of Northerners, including myself, can agree with. Our big war was a family quarrel—far, far worse than a normal family quarrel, I grant you—but, North or South, we are all Americans. Though my father is an officer of the present administration, I regret that President Johnson's party is treating the South so harshly.'

Dacers noted her downcast expression and the unmistakable melancholy in her eyes. For an instant, her face reflected so much that was good in her character: her broad compassion; her desire to see her country's recent wounds healed and the folk of North and South united in the quest for the bright future America promised. In that instant, he realised how much he admired her sterling qualities—no, how much he *loved* her.

He quickly turned his attention to the next portion of the first newspaper announcement: *'The ban not con.'*

'Ah, I see—that obviously means the banner is not conquered and it sounds suspiciously like a call to arms, the same sort of dodge the Dixie Ghosts tried; a money making fraud based on a spurious move to re-start the American Civil War. I can't believe anyone would try that again so soon after the

Ghosts were tossed into jail. The case was widely reported in the papers.'

'Well, it is certainly some kind of organisation to do with the Confederacy', said Roberta. 'And it announces that a meeting is to be called soon. I puzzled over the meaning of the initials LUB for a long time then I matched the initials against Father Ryan's poem and hit on League of the Unconquered Banner.'

'Sounds reasonable enough,' said Dacers. 'How about the combination of letters at the end, the Si Se Ty that looks almost Chinese?'

'I was puzzled by that for a long time, too,' she said. 'Then I recalled that, as he jumped to the stage of Ford's Theatre after shooting President Lincoln, John Wilkes Booth shouted the motto of his native State, Virginia: *Sic Semper Tyrannis—Thus To All Tyrants.* After I juggled with those initials for a time, the slogan suddenly came to me and it set the seal on the whole thing as having something to do with the old Confederacy, with Booth's cry as a kind of motto.'

'Very good reasoning and it strengthens my uncomfortable feeling that it is an echo of the Dixie Ghosts' case,' he said. 'The announcement in today's paper takes us a little further.' He began to trace each word with his finger. 'See? We have the same trappings; the initials LUB, and the initials representing Booth's cry, signing off and, between them the message: *Mtg arrgd. 7-30pm Fri inst T Rm Crem Gdns.*

Roberta looked at the paper more closely.

'I understand the main gist of it, saying a meeting has been arranged but the last bit about the venue escapes me,' she said.

'It wouldn't if you were a native Londoner,' he said. 'That scrap of code: *T Rm, Crem Gdns,* simply means Big Tea Room, Cremorne Gardens. So that's where our mysterious friends are meeting at 7-30 pm on Friday—three nights from now.'

'Cremorne Gardens?' Roberta gasped, 'Isn't that the notorious place beside the Thames at Chelsea?'

Dacers smiled. 'Notorious is the right word but Cremorne Pleasure Gardens have a double life. They put on a very respectable face in the mornings and afternoons. Parents quite happily take their children there to see the animals in the menagerie, ride the merry-go-rounds, watch the ascents of daring balloonists or drink ginger-pop.

'Towards evening, the character of the place changes. The wine, gin, whisky and grog flows in quantity. Certain types of men and women who live mainly at night make their appearance, replacing doting parents and their innocent offspring. Need I say more?'

Roberta had been listening to him with eyes wide open and her mouth making an "O". She was displaying what Dacers thought of as her "tomboy" side which was every bit as attractive as her compassionate side—and every bit as loveable.

'How fascinating Cremorne Gardens must be. I should like to go there one evening,' she said. 'My father is always saying I should see more of London.'

Dacers started. 'Oh, no, not if I can help it! Cremorne is no place for a single young lady on her own. There are pitfalls and I'm certain your father did not have Cremorne in mind when he said you should see more of London,'

'You make it sound very forbidding. I suppose I'll go there without any fear when I am a fully operating detective and I feel I am well on my way to achieving that ambition.'

Dacers stood with his head on one side, regarding her with a quizzical expression. 'What brings you to that conclusion?' he asked.

'Why, my dear sir. Did you not witness the ease with which I translated that first newspaper notice into understandable form? I probably have a natural talent for breaking down clues.' Her eyes were sparkling with a whimsical light familiar to him from across the breakfast table.

'What ease?' he countered, half teasing. 'You admitted you struggled with the puzzle and I think it was your knowledge of modern American poetry that did the work for you when you spotted the link with Father Ryan. You might qualify as a professor of literature, but that's hardly the same as a detective.' Even as he spoke, he realised how patronising he sounded. She had displayed a sharp, investigative mind and he, man like, had to belittle her. All at once, he saw himself from the woman's viewpoint—from Roberta's viewpoint—and he perceived that the male of the species always gave a woman's achievement short shrift just because it was the accomplishment of a woman. It seemed almost a duty in this society which Roberta had justifiably complained was male dominated.

What gave him qualms of most regret, however, was the thought that he had hurt Roberta and that was something he would never consciously do. Yet again, he thought how very deeply he loved her with his one-sided love which he believed she would never return.

She pretended to pout. 'Oh, fie! You have quite deflated me just when I thought I had taken a great step towards proving that ladies are brainy enough to be detectives.'

'Oh, you've done valuable work,' he said with much more genuine feeling. 'You've done some remarkable brain work and established that there is a group here in England called the League of the Unconquered Banner—or some similar name—which appears to be associated with the old Confederacy. We don't know its aims. The Dixie Ghosts were criminal and dangerous but we don't know what these people are up to. Maybe they're quite innocent. If not, the British authorities and your Ambassador, Mr. Adams, need to know. A good deal of investigating must be done to be sure of being on safe ground.'

'Oh, good! How I'd enjoy being involved in an investigation just to prove that my instincts as a detective are sound,' said Roberta. Her eyes were bright with enthusiasm and she was obviously gripped by her tomboy mood.

Dacers sighed. 'My dear lady, please be assured that I shall not take you on as a partner in this matter. The affair of the Dixie Ghosts turned nasty to the point where I was almost fed to the fishes in the Thames. If this new affair turns out to be dangerous and you are injured or killed it would break your father's heart. I respect him very much and I know you mean everything to him. You are fortunate to have each other.'

This appeal to her deepest sentiments had its effect.

She was touched by Dacers' concern for her father and she recalled the long hours of anxiety when she nursed him through his close brush with death. Then the fervent sense of thanksgiving when he came out of his fevers and gathered strength and she knew she would have her wise, gentle and beloved father a little longer. Her answer was slow in coming, but when it did, there was nothing of her reckless, tomboyish style in it.

'I suppose you're right, Mr. Dacers. I tend to get carried away by my enthusiasms. In all my time in England, I never learned to be a contented woman of the English type, happy to settle down with a romantic novel or my needlework.'

Dacers smiled. 'You should try it sometime, just to keep out of mischief. However, I know the Van Trasks were among America's earliest Dutch settlers, so I suppose you'll always want to see what's over the next hill.'

'Ah, that sounds as if you understand my inquisitiveness,' she said. 'It's most likely a family trait, going back for centuries. I was probably born to be a detective.'

'Possibly. Maybe Professor Darwin, can give you an explanation all based on evolution but please curb your inherited enthusiasm in this matter of Cremorne Gardens—there could be danger lurking there.'

'Danger?' she said as if savouring the word. 'After doing nothing special all winter, the prospect of some excitement is tempting me to abandon my newly made plans concerning romantic novels and needlework.'

'No, Stick to those civilised plans', he said firmly. 'And leave the meeting at Cremorne to me.'

She looked at him with a light in her eyes that seemed partly mocking and partly whimsical. Dacers hoped it did not betoken a stirring of her streak of tomboy defiance?

CHAPTER 6

A REFUGE FOR THE BOX

The day after Mr. O stood beside the Thames at Chelsea, surrounded by scented tobacco smoke and smitten by a new notion for getting the box from Birkenhead off his hands to evade any police sweep for it, he walked boldly along Southampton Row. Under his left arm he carried the cumbersome box, wrapped in a substantial covering of canvas. O was at that time occupying a set of small but adequate rooms in Putney, the district in which he was seeking a suitable house for his cousin-bride and himself after their marriage. He did not wish the box to be found there but he was on his way to a place where it could be comfortably lodged away from prying eyes.

O understood that it contained something of extreme interest and value to serious collectors of Americana. Almost certainly, its theft had caused a fuss up north but he was confident that it would be safe where he hoped to leave it until he thought of a profitable way to dispose of it.

A policeman was plodding towards him at the usual foot patrol pace and, as they drew level O took an impudent pleasure in addressing him.

'Good morning, Constable. Another promising day, what?'

The officer saluted. 'Good morning, sir. Yes, it feels a bit like spring.'

Walking on, O smiled and thought of the value of a dandyish costume and a handsome walking stick when carrying stolen property under the noses of the police. Had he appeared to be a poor man or even a labouring man, he could expect a gruff question from the peeler: 'Just a moment. What're you carrying under your arm?'

O continued a little way down Southampton Row then he turned off at a straggling street lined with old houses, many in a State of decay. Deep in the street was a large building of the tenement type, every bit as run-down as the neighbouring property. It had an ornamental entrance over which moulded letters declared it to be *"Marlborough Dwellings"*.

Although it was inhabited by those managing to make ends meet rather than the truly poor, the truly poor had left their mark on the premises. The building was bereft of the impressive wooden doors it must once have had. In exceptionally cold winters, the street-dwelling truly poor had a habit of raiding vulnerable properties for firewood and street doors often disappeared.

Consequently, the entrance hall of Marlborough Dwellings was quite unprotected from the open street and its denizens.

O climbed the set of cracked stone steps and entered the hallway and then mounted a creaking inner stairway.

In a small room on the first floor, a young man was seated at a table cluttered with materials of painting and drawing. His surroundings were far from luxurious. A single bed, unmade, stood in one corner; another corner was occupied by an easel bearing a large, blank canvas and, behind these a small and grubby window let in thin shafts of light, hopelessly inadequate as an aid to painting, Here and there, oddments of clothing, books and boxes were scattered about.

Adolphus Crayford, sitting at the table, was working on a metal plate, which had a whitened surface. On this, he was drawing a number of horsemen. When his boldly drawn lines were etched into the plate, it would be an illustration for a "penny dreadful", one of the shockingly bloodthirsty cheap magazines. The vociferous reformers of British morals claimed such publications were causing the reformatories and prisons to be filled with boys and young men, corrupted by them.

Adolphus had his heart set on higher art but sweated hackwork was all he could get to keep the wolf from the door.

A sharp rap on the door caused him to turn his head and without any bidding from him, the door opened and the face of the man Adolphus knew as 'Mr. O' looked around it, grinning.

He looked the very picture of the amiable chum calling in to share some of the spirit of this bright morning in a little chat. He turned on a flow of charm as if it was obtainable from a tap.

'Good morning, young Mr. Crayford,' he hailed. 'So good to see you gainfully employed.'

Adolphus, son of a hard working vicar of a poor country parish in Dorset, turned his lean face towards his cheerful visitor. It was the face of a young man who was being handed a hard time by life.

'Not so gainful,' he said dolefully. 'Do you realise the fetching and carrying I have to do for these shark publishers? I have to collect the prepared plates and the copy to be illustrated from St Giles. The drawings must be ready two weeks before publication day and, when they are finished, I have to trudge over to Seven Dials to have them engraved and march back to the printer with them and collect fresh plates for the next round of slavery. I walk all London because the printer won't employ a errand boy and I'm keeping alive on bread and cheese.' He paused in his doleful litany for a moment then asked O, hopefully: 'Anything in the wind?'

'Sad to say, old chap, nothing. In all my acquaintance with the cream of this city's finest painters—which, as you know, is considerable—I never knew a situation like the present one. Not one seeks a studio assistant. Mr. Whistler, just back from his adventures in the Americas, is looking for commissions. Mr. Sandys is not doing too badly but can't run to a salary for an assistant and Mr. Rossetti is in one of his gloomy moods and is scarcely painting at all. But, cheer up, old fellow, spring is nearly here. It's bound to bring a change.'

Adolphus shrugged and asked: 'What is that bundle you're lugging around under your arm?'

'This?' said O as if he had just remembered that he still had the canvas-wrapped bundle under his arm. 'This is the real reason I called on you. You know I'm to marry later in the year and that I deal in oddments of curios. Well, since I'm living in a couple rooms in Putney and have no storeroom or showroom and must quit my rooms when I get married, I'm asking a few friends to look after some oddments of stock I was keeping in my rooms. When I'm married, I'll have a regular place of business. I'm sure you won't mind looking after this box for a little while. It contains just a few hobby items—you know, the kind of things that interest people who go in for birds' eggs and foreign coins.'

'No, I don't mind in the least,' Adolphus said. 'If you move those few books in the far corner, there'll be room for it.'

O moved the books and laid the box in the corner then took out his smoking materials and lit up another of his scented cigarettes. He gulped in smoke and proceeded to fill the room with the sickly pungency of the tobacco, which Adolphus greatly disliked. He also disliked O's habit of discarding the tiny scrap left of one cigarette on his floor before immediately lighting another. Adolphus was not sure that he really liked Mr. O or his brash style of boosting his own self-importance but O had done him a good turn and he believed one good turn deserved another.

Had he known the truth about O's 'good turn' he would certainly have felt differently.

Adolphus wanted a career as an artist and he had undoubted talent. His father's living did not produce the wherewithal to send him to art school but the young man saved enough money to go to London to try to further his ambitions. He found the city hideous yet attractive; bright but gloomy; welcoming but threatening. It was a place where flamboyant wealth flourished beside the most abject poverty. He often regretted leaving his father's parish with its green fields in sight of the sea but he persevered in his uneasy affair with London because, for all its faults, the city had a verve and vitality all its own and sent out a challenge to all young men of ambition.

It was, however, never easy for any poor young man, no matter how talented or how high his ambitions, to discover a suitable career without being championed by some highly placed person.

Adolphus found hack-work in the St Giles' colony of cheap printers and hack writers. It kept him busy for hour after hour and only just paid for his shabby lodging and meagre food. When he could snatch some time away from his drudgery, he would try to find some better employment.

Ideally, he hoped he might be taken on as studio assistant by an established painter to grind colours, mix paints, do general studio chores and fetch and carry in exchange for some tuition. One evening he paid a visit to a noted tavern in the region of Charlotte Street where there was a cluster of artists' studios. It was the drinking place of a number of famed brothers of the brush as well as hopeful daubers and hangers-on to the artistic community.

He took a portfolio of six water colours, mostly done in his pre-London days before drudgery claimed him. He hoped they might catch the attention of someone who could offer a helping hand and a dandyish fellow standing by the bar saw the portfolio, went over to Adolphus and asked if he might see his work. He said he was 'a kind of general factotum' around the artistic community and generally known as O or Owl.

O looked at the pictures with interest and declared that they showed great promise. He looked at them a second time in what appeared to be professional style with his eyes half closed.

'You know, old chap, the whole six would look capital on my bedroom wall,' he said. 'Would you care to sell them to me?' He mentioned a price. It was a modest price but Adolphus, always in need of extra cash, accepted at once.

O carried them away happily, as well he might be for he had noticed two attractive facts about the pictures. Firstly, doubtless by the sheerest chance, without any conscious copying, the country lad's style was remarkably like that of the French water-colourist Octave Drax, who was very much in fashion. Secondly, Adolphus had not signed the paintings so they did not finish up on O's bedroom wall. O, master of many black arts, exercised one of them—forgery. Eventually, the half-dozen pictures, each inscribed with a near perfect 'Octave Drax', went to an easily gulled collector for a handsome sum to the benefit of O's pocket.

O cultivated the friendship of Adolphus Crayford, telling him would watch for a vacancy for a studio assistant among the many eminent artists he knew. His true motive for the cultivation was to discover whether Adolphus had any other work that could be transmuted into paintings apparently from the hand of Drax or, for that matter, any sufficiently like that of any noted painter on which O might profitably work his dark magic.

O had a long experience of dubious dealings and he had always believed in taking his time on a project when it seemed the best course. Rather than rush in the matter of viewing Crayford's back collection and arouse the young man's suspicions, He would play the good, breezy chum until his chance came.

In the meantime, he was satisfied that nobody among those seeking a valuable artefact stolen in the north of England would ever imagine that it was squirreled away in the obscurity of a poverty stricken artist's apartment in far off London, lost among the capital's teeming citizens?

That same day, among that sea of people, a handful whose fortunes would eventually become entangled were busy with their individual concerns. Roberta Van Trask who, a short a short time before had admitted she had little time for the genteel hobby of needlework was plying a needle, altering a garment. An observer might have noted a certain expectant light in her eyes that could suggest she was anticipating some excitement to come. Esther, her level-headed black maid and companion who was more a sister than a servant, was looking on worriedly. Every so often, she murmured 'I don't think you should be doing this. It can only lead to trouble.'

Lodging in the home of a British supporter of the Georgian General who had conceived a grotesque plan for what he imagined was the post-war betterment of his State, two of the General's right hand men were busy finalising plans to for a meeting in Cremorne Gardens. They hoped this would be fruitful because earlier setbacks had burdened them with anxiety about their inability to discover a certain stolen box as well as a missing man, the General's third emissary who had a lame foot.

CHAPTER 7

GRANDON'S BURDEN OF TROUBLE

The man with the lame foot was not far from Sadler and Dobbs. He was in a back room in the home of a cousin in Somers Town, a little way behind the big railway terminal of Euston and not a great distance from Camden Town where Sadler and Dobbs were lodging with the maker of breech-loading rifles. He was brooding over several setbacks. There was the failure of his attempt on the life of Septimus Dacers; there was the loss of a Remington pistol which he had used in several military engagements across the Atlantic and, most worrying of all, there was the loss of the horse he had hired from a livery stable, swept away in the fury of the cattle stampede.

A horse, plus the saddle and tackle hired with it, amounted to a substantial cost. A lavish amount of the portion of ready cash with which he absconded from Sadler and Dobbs went on the smart clothing forming a disguise in his murder attempt. Now, Grandon was feeling the financial pinch. There was also the precarious nature of the position he had put himself into.

The owner of the livery stable was an ugly, pugnacious man who looked very likely to be familiar with "the Fancy", the community whose interests were racehorses, fighting dogs, cockfights and bare fisted prize-fighting. He had wanted ex-Sergeant Ned Grandon's name and address when he hired out the horse and Grandon gave him false ones. He had banked on there not being an immediate hue and cry after his shooting of Dacers and that he could make a hasty escape back to the stable and return his mount. Then, in some convenient alley, he would strip off his beard, discard his spurs and his distinguishing billycock hat and substitute a cap he kept in his pocket. He might then easily make his way to Somers Town on foot. He could not disguise his limp but witnesses who saw him shoot from the saddle would not know about it and would remember his black beard as his chief characteristic.

From the start, Grandon's strategy had risks but he had not reckoned on everything going wrong due to a stampede of cattle, something he might encounter on the developing cattle ranges of the American West but which he never expected to burst upon a London street. On losing himself in the warren of small streets and alleys after the stampede, he got rid of the beard, spurs and billycock, donned the cap and found his way back to his relative's home without mishap. Then his doubts began to assail him.

Ned Grandon was no coward but, from whichever angle he looked at his present position, he saw he was in a hole. He even wondered if he was not a little crazy to have put himself in that position in the first place. Maybe his experiences in the war had unhinged him. It had happened to plenty of other men. He was overtaken by thoughts that jarred him back to solid, sane reality as he skulked in his Somers Town refuge. The more he brooded on his actions of the recent past, the more unnerved he became and the more he convinced himself that they were the doings of a crazed man.

If he had been in his right mind, he would never have sought to avenge his brother's downfall by killing Septimus Dacers in the way he chose. He secretly schemed for months; he curried favour with General Vavasour to gain a place with Sadler and Dobbs on their expedition to England specifically to seek Dacers and kill him and he made a hectic runaway flight from Liverpool to London. Yet, in the end, the murder plot blew back in his face.

His multiple problems were now nagging him persistently: suppose the liveryman tracked him down, demanding the price of his horse and tackle. Such a man was likely to inhabit a social milieu from which he could call on the support of prize-fighting friends who might take a perverse pleasure in beating a man to a pulp!

In the way that imaginary bogeymen can almost become real and haunt a fevered mind, this notion began to prey on him.

Then there was the worry that, in spite of his elaborate efforts at disguise, Dacers' reports of an attempt on his life might cause the police to discover him!

Worrying, too, were the undisguised hints concerning money from his cousin, Hector, with whom he was lodging. Hector had tolerated him as a visiting relative but the toleration soon grew very thin. Hector he had a wife and a growing family and was simply a working man. He had lately dropped broad hints that Grandon could not expect to live rent free for ever in the household of a mere artisan.

In his youth, Grandon had spent some time living with Hector's parents and he and Hector were old cronies from their young days but relations between the two were now becoming strained. Money was at the root of their mutual ill-feeling and Grandon had lately come to the alarming realisation that the modest portion of the General's funding with which he fled to London, was almost dried up. He did not realise it but his problems were bulking up and preying on his mind. In a word unknown until the next century, he was becoming paranoid.

The big war in America had its effects on both Hector and Grandon in different ways. Ned Grandon was most drastically affected through his military service with the Confederacy. Hector, was happy to be on the make provided it was within wide margins of safety. He had hoped he might receive some small financial benefit from the ambitious post-war confidence trick put in motion by Ned's brother, Howard. Howard, in the persona of "Mr. Fortune", was the deviser and leader of the 'Dixie Ghosts.' These tricksters arrived in England with elaborate plans to rook the British profiteers who had supplied ships, armaments and other goods to the South during the American Civil War.

With an unlikely tale that the defeated South was gearing to rise in arms again and required money for its war aims, they had managed to relieve some of the most gullible of the old suppliers of yet more money.

It ended in disaster and Howard Grandon—otherwise "Mr. Fortune"—was now in a British convict prison. While his brother fought the powerful armies of Abraham Lincoln as an honourable Southern soldier, Howard Grandon established himself in the Confederate capital, Richmond, Virginia. He had a minor post in the Confederate government then became a double agent, frequently crossing the Potomac River between Virginia and the Union capital, Washington, in disguise and dealing with both sides. He was never caught and made such a profitable thing of his duplicity that, while America endured its post-war turmoil, he resolved he would exploit the situation and follow a life of crime.

With the collapse of the Southern government, Howard Grandon knew, from his days inside the Government apparatus where he could find details of the British interests and individuals who had contributed to keeping the lifeblood of the rebel nation flowing by trafficking in ships, arms, ammunition, food and other supplies. He appropriated these for use in his confidence trick, founded on a tale of a bogus resurgent South, already re-arming itself and ready to fight all over again.

His brother, Ned, had knowledge of the scheme from his brother's glowing, supremely confident letters. Remaining in Georgia, Ned had no hand in implementing the trick Howard had dreamed up but became part of General Vavasour's hare-brained Unconquered Banner movement which had spread its wings and was established in a tentative way in England.

Like his cousin Hector, in London, who knew of the Dixie Ghosts' villainy, Ned vainly hoped some of the money conjured out of the shipbuilders and armaments kings across the ocean by Howard's tricksters would come his way. The Grandons in both England and America had never been rich and saw no reason why they should not benefit from the rooking of a bunch of money hungry manufacturers and speculators who had chased profits during the war in America.

The spectacular collapse of the Dixie Ghosts and the trials of the principal actors in their crimes were reported in the newspapers in full. It emerged from press clippings sent to Ned by his cousin Hector that the enquiry agent Septimus Dacers, of Bloomsbury, played an active role in bringing them to justice. In fact, Dacers was played up in print as a hero of the debacle that brought an end to the Dixie Ghosts' criminal venture. The trial judge had made special mention of Dacers' energetic unmasking of the man who called himself "Mr. Fortune", chief of the Dixie Ghosts.

Septimus Dacers loomed in Ned Grandon's imagination as the *bete noir* who who had ruined the chances of his London relatives and himself falling into some little profit in the way of some crumbs from the rich table furnished by the Dixie Ghosts' villainly.

Ned Grandon, was a Southerner who, like so many more, had in no way profited from his service to the Confederacy. He had gained only near destitution, permanent physical impairment, an exhausted spirit and a burning sense of injustice. Possibly, as he now came suspect, he was not wholly mentally balanced after his war experiences and he focussed his resentment on Septimus Dacers, of Bloomsbury. He was convinced that, had the applecart of his brother's confidence trick not been so decisively upset by Dacers, he would be enjoying a share of the easy life.

After four years in the hellish American Civil War he had developed a lowered tolerance to the notion of killing a fellow human being, so he decided to go to London and kill Dacers. After all, he had lived in London for a time when young. He knew the city fairly well and his cousin's modest home in Somers Town might be used as a bolthole.

He was sure Hector and his family would put him up but he would not make them privy to his murderous scheme, so no blame could be attached to them if his plans failed. If he could plan and execute the deed skilfully enough, all London, including Hector and his family, would only know that the murder of Septimus Dacers was the work of an unknown hand.

In preparation, he acquired an up-to-date directory of city businesses and found private inquiry agents, including Dacers, listed. He observed the address from the small park in the middle of the square for a couple of mornings, saw Dacers come out to post his letters and followed him, keeping well behind him, noting where he crossed the larger street every morning to reach the post box.

On the morning after his failed attempt on Dacers life, when sobering thoughts occupied him, he was faced by Hector over breakfast which was always early because Hector had to leave early to follow his trade as a carpenter. Cousin Ned was an American relative and everyone knew American relatives were always turning up in the old country heavily laden with money, usually just in time to save the old folks at home from eviction or bankruptcy. It was a stock theme of the popular melodramas staged in the cheap theatres known as "penny gaffs".

Ned had shown up out of the blue having arrived in England on some mission he had not discussed with Hector and his family but, so far, he had shown not one red cent of any fabulous American wealth.

Hector was not tight-fisted but money was not easily obtained by a man in his social position. He had the broad hospitality of the London working-class and an honest Cockney outspokenness. That outspokenness showed itself over the breakfast table.

'You know, Cousin Ned, keepin' a family alive these days ain't easy', he said bluntly when his wife, Sarah, had left the table to go to the kitchen. 'What I mean to say is, you comes an' goes most of the day but I don't ask what you're up to. It ain't none of my business but I presumes you might be makin' a copper or two—an' spendin' a bit. Like on that sharp toff's set of togs, billycock tile and all, you showed up in. That must've cost you a fair slice of gelt. You don't never seem to think of coughing up a few quid to keep this house goin', do you?'

His cousin's words brought home to Grandon the uncomfortable truth that the modest amount of money he took with him when he abandoned Sadler and Dobbs had dwindled away alarmingly. He could scarcely account for its disappearance and, before long, he might well be penniless here in London with no means of earning so much as a copper. He knew he must part with a little more money. Though his stomach sank at the prospect, he tried to hold up an untroubled front.

'Of course, you are right, Cousin Hector. It's not that I had the slightest intention of sponging on you. It was all a mere matter of my having a lapse of memory. I'll bring down a few pounds for you when I go up to my room later.'

Hector nodded and mumbled his thanks. He seemed satisfied for the present.

Ned Grandon felt a hollow void in his guts and a coldness at his brow. He felt his grasp on reality was floundering and a jittery apprehension was encroaching on him. In short, he was close to a nervous crack-up.

CHAPTER 8

A FUSS AT CREMORNE

A skyrocket whizzed into the chilly air, trailing an arc of smoke then, high above Chelsea, it burst, releasing a near-blinding cascade of red, green and blue sparks giving the evening air a brief fairyland touch. Such displays would soon give James Whistler, the cantankerous painter, who lived nearby, the inspiration to paint sky high flowering lights. He captured in paint the hissing, exploding and descending colours that regularly emanated from rowdy and unprincipled Cremorne Gardens, the pleasure spot on the Thames.

Whistler found the gardens excitingly attractive, as did many a man about town, many a dandified lounger of the Swell Mob and many a sharp-faced luminary of the Flash Mob, London's two major regiments of cunning criminality. Then there were dollimops from the houses of fleshly pleasure in gaudy finery, the property of their madams. Their less favoured, streetwalking sisters, sometimes marked by their pimps' fists as well as by the signs of hunger, were also to be found at Cremorne. At the bottom of Cremorne's social order were the scroungers: the ragged folk with tales of distress who had somehow eluded the gardens' security measures along with barefoot urchins who scampered among the patrons, begging pennies.

Though it was still winter and Cremorne was not going at full pelt, the gardens still displayed their bawdy vulgarity and Septimus Dacers felt its power the minute he paid his money and entered at the 'Water Entrance', opposite the river. He had been here before, professionally, in the company of the police and Cremorne's joviality and lighthearted sense, tainted though it was, never failed to touch him.

In truth he had little enough to be light-hearted about for, when his cab reached the Water Entrance, he was already late for the scheduled LUB meeting. A cart had overturned on Cheney Row, blocking the way to the entrance to the gardens and the usual altercation between cabbie and carter began. A policeman arrived and more or less settled their quarrel then took his time questioning the pair and writing up the facts of the case in his notebook after which Dacers helped all three to right the cart.

He hastened towards the Big Tea Room at the further end of the gardens. He hurried by paths lit by Chinese lanterns in the bare trees above them. He ignored the smirks and winks of the dollimops who strolled the paths at a snail's pace and he turned a deaf ear to a man at a red hot brazier hoarsely announcing baked potatoes.

He passed an open pavilion where mulled ale was on sale and a group of young men with top hats askew swung pint pots and sang in uncertain harmony a raucous gem from the music halls:

> *'I'm a chickaleery bloke*
> *Hackney is the town*
> *That I was born in.*
> *And, if you wants to*
> *Catch me out, you've*
> *Got to get up early*
> *In the mornin'*

He kept a steady pace onward, hearing the thumping drum and brassy blare of a German band, somewhere ahead, keeping fresh the memory of the long departed summer when it thumped and blared through hot and lazy days. He passed one of the features of the gardens that still brought outraged cluckings from elderly puritans who remembered when the waltz was considered immoral, Cremorne's Dancing Platform, a spacious, raised floor, was closed up now for winter. When brighter weather returned, it would provide a colourful and lively spectacle of whirling crinolines and flying coattails as the younger generations revived both the waltz and the polka.

He came in sight of the Big Tea Room which advertised itself as a great splash of bright light on the landscape. It was a glass structure, influenced by the vogue in glass buildings after the creation of the Crystal Palace in Hyde Park for the Great Exhibition of 1851. The interior was brightly lit and the glass panes which made up the walls permitted him to see a busy scene of numerous parties seated at long tables. There were a great many of these long tables and it was the custom for various private parties to be in progress at them nightly. Wedding parties; engagement parties; birthday parties; parties for those leaving for the colonies and for those just returned went on amid large, steaming tea urns and plates piled high with cakes, tarts and muffins.

It was a remarkable fact that, although so many partygoers from various social classes roistered within one space and plenty of strong drink was consumed, there was no clashing of parties. Each remained a self-contained entity and, although a shared heartiness reigned in the great room, one party never interfered with another. Much criticised Cremorne, it seemed, had the ability to level the classes and promote harmony, despite all the critics' cries that the pleasure gardens were a blot on the fair face of Chelsea.

As Dacers entered the premises, he felt himself immediately wrapped around by its warmth and the welcoming aroma of hot food. The various parties were in full swing at their tables which were interspersed by cast-iron standards, moulded and painted to represent heavily foliaged trees. From a distance, he quickly spotted a table surrounded by a group of males some of whom had subtle touches to their clothing—a broad-brimmed hat here; a string tie instead of a full British style cravat there, which marked them as Americans. Others were obviously British men of affairs: quite likely businessmen, manufacturers, speculators and capitalists in a great or small way of business.

Such a collection of men struck a familiar chord in Dacers' memory and brought back uneasy recollections of the previous day's assassination attempt, He felt sure the hand of the defeated Dixie Ghosts was in that attempt. And now he felt sure the LUB also had something to do with the Ghosts. This audience had the look of those whom the Ghosts' hoped to fleece of their money. Some were exiles from America who had supported the South; others were agents of arms companies and suppliers of other essential goods who supported the warring Southerners through the blockade—breaking system of smuggling. Surely, a revived set of Ghosts were not trying the same trick of rook the old blockade breakers of funds with the tale of a revitalised South needing money to start hostilities all over again!

As he drew nearer, he saw that the gathering was listening raptly to a tall man standing before them. He, too, had the un-mistakable appearance of an American in his long dark topcoat and his wide hat. His lean frame and hollow cheeks, reminded Dacers of pictures of Confederate soldiers he had seen. Dacers gave a grunt of annoyance, realising that, while he had set off in time, the mishap with the cart in the road had caused him to miss the opening of the meeting.

The orator was too far away for him to hear what he was saying so he put on an unsteady wobble and pushed his tall hat over his eyes, becoming a Cremorne type: the lonely drinker who usually finished his evening by being discovered sound asleep in a chair in some remote region of the gardens.

He edged his way towards of the fringe of the body being addressed by the rangy man of Southern rebel appearance. In doing so, he noticed a second man, slender, loose-limbed and costumed in similar style to the orator, sitting at the front of the audience, none of whom noticed Dacers take up an empty chair, position it at the back of the gathering and sit down. He continued his pose as a tipsy idler, hat tipped over his eyes and seemingly asleep. He watched the speaker through half closed eyes.

The man's strong voice betrayed his place of origin with a slow drawl, what he was saying with a considerable depth of emotion, sounded very strange to Dacers.

'…It might come as news to many of you English folks that, back in those days, when the colonies were gathering around George Washington and increasingly of a mind to break with the Crown, Georgia showed reluctance to get involved and took a long time about it.

'When it did join the rebel colonies, it did not disregard the numerous Englishmen who helped create Georgia and brought benefits to it. They cast the mould in which we who call ourselves Georgia Crackers—descendants of the first colonists—are cast. Soon after we became a State we honoured many of these men for they supported our bid for liberty in spite of their king and Parliament and a vast number of their fellow citizens.'

Dacers was immediately startled by what the man was saying. Among his first words was the name of Georgia which at once brought the recollection of the Remington revolver dropped by the man who attempted to kill him and the faintly scratched lettering on its butt, recording the name of a Georgia infantry regiment. Surely there must be a connection between the man who fired on him and these visitors who identified themselves as Georgians. He listened with acute interest as the man seemed to be developing a history of Georgia and its relationship with Great Britain.

'One of our earliest acts was to name a number of our counties after those inspiring men,' he was saying. 'First, the British soldier, General James Oglethorpe, the founder of Georgia, which he created as a colony to give British convicts and debtors a fresh chance in life. He was humane man, which is more than can be said for those calling the tune in Georgia today. There was Chatham county, for the Earl of Chatham, a champion of American Liberty and Burke County for Edmund Burke, Irish born, a noble light of the British Parliament and one of Europe's great political thinkers.

'We created Wilkes County to honour John Wilkes, Member of Parliament and fearless agitator for liberty and Glynn County for John Glynn, Member of Parliament, friend of Wilkes and the lawyer who defended Wilkes when he was hauled before the courts. There were others, ladies and gentlemen. We might have fought British soldiers in our War of Independence and that of 1812 but we would never cast from our gratitude, respect and affection those from across the Atlantic who, like you, were our friends. As the poem says, our banner must be furled but those sentiments of gallantry and love of our native soil which it embodies and which we share with our spiritual kinsman the British will never pass away.

'There are plenty of people in Georgia who are rightly proud of their British background. Why, our own leader, the General, comes from an old established family which came into England from France with William the Conqueror. And while mentioning the General, I know that you folks are from several parts of this country but most are from London. I wonder if any of you know of a certain Mr. O who resides somewhere in London. He has something the General wishes to acquire, something of importance to our objective. If anyone knows where this Mr. O can be found, kindly let Sergeant Major Dobbs or myself—'

Dacers made another mental note. The speaker had given a military rank to his companion and he had the mien of a war-hardened old soldier himself. Again, the memory of the legend with its military connotation scratched on the butt of the pistol came to his mind. It named a Georgia militia and this man harped so much on Georgia that he must surely come from that State.

The speaker's oration had suddenly ceased because of a loud creaking sound behind him. He whirled and saw one of the cast iron 'trees' rocking back and forth on its stand, as if about to fall at any moment. Those sitting nearest began to rise and hurry out of the way and Dacers saw that the movement revealed a startled young man standing behind the tree. He was slender in a long overcoat and a tall hat that seemed too big for him. He must have bumped or nudged the tree by accident, caused it to shift and reveal his presence. He clutched it, trying to keep it upright but to no avail.

The cast-iron tree teetered forward then back again, hitting the flustered young man's hat and knocking it back on his head. This fully revealed an oval face; a young woman's face—that of Roberta Van Trask!

Septimus Dacers almost jumped out of his skin and stood up quickly just as the iron tree swung forward again, completely off balance, hitting the tiled floor and shattering to bits.

Somebody shouted: 'It's a young fellow, spying on us!'

'No!' shouted someone else. 'It's a girl!'

Dacers saw Roberta turn and run just as a knot of men from the meeting rose quickly and started after her. From her hiding place, she reached the pathway between several long tables laden with cakes, buns and huge tea urns. She was dressed in an outlandish collection of clothing which did little to disguise her femininity: the long overcoat, what seemed to be some form of trousers and the oversized tall hat which she held on to grimly as she ran.

She had a good lead on the men following her and Dacers put a spurt on, coming up behind the group chasing her. He came into their midst and they took him to be one of themselves. He shoved a couple out of his way by brute force, tripped another and was then clear of them, He came alongside one of the long tables which had a large, steaming tea urn at its end. He paused momentarily, grabbed the porcelain handle of the urn's tap and hauled the large brass vessel off the table just as the pursuers were almost on him.

A great surge of hot tea splashed up as it hit the floor and the pursuers found themselves floundering through a tide of it. They halted in confusion for a short time, howling and swearing at Dacers' back as he continued running after the girl.

She was keeping up a good pace and she was nearing the wide door of the Big Tea Room. Dacers knew that Cremorne Gardens were unknown territory to her and she would not know where to go once she was outside the refreshment room. There was very little doubt that her energy would soon give out and Dacers was beginning to feel twinges of pain in the side that was once injured by the knife of Dandy Jem the Swell Mobsman. He could hear the irate runners coming hard, having gathered themselves together again.

He closed on Roberta just as she reached the door. Panting, he called to her:

'Keep running out of the—door. You'll see a—big hedge straight ahead—make for it.'

She was startled to find he was running beside her and she half-turned her head.

'Where did—you come – from?' she panted.

'Never mind. Just run.'

They were outside now in in the sharp air of the night which was dark, moonless and with a touch of winter mist coming up from the river. They were running along one of Cremorne's many paths, the pursuers were not far behind and both were beginning to feel they would soon be sapped of energy.

The large hedge loomed ahead of them. It was neatly trimmed and obviously enclosed a spacious area. There was a wide opening and a path giving access to the dark, mysterious area behind the hedge. Dacers could see that Roberta was slackening speed and labouring for breath as heavily as himself. He put his hand on her back and pushed her forward towards the gap in the hedge.

'In there—quick!' he gasped with what felt like the last of his breath.

The girl almost stumbled along the pathway and vaguely realised that the path ran between two privet hedges and, so far as she could see anything, she had the impression that there were more such hedges around them and before them.

'Where—are we?' she gulped.

The pounding boots of the pursuers sounded ominously near their place of refuge.

'At the entrance to—the maze', gasped Dacers, putting his hands on her shoulders to stop her running then pushing her down to the path.

'Quick—get down there—take your hat off—' he instructed breathlessly, 'Lie at the bottom of the hedge and off the path—if there's any clearance under the hedge, roll under it—keep still down in the dark.'

She grasped his meaning at once as the hubbub of the running men grew nearer. She snatched off her tall hat, held it close to her body and dropped down, found a strip of earth between the hard path and the hedge and flattened out on it.

Frighteningly near, the sound of pursuing feet mounted and a gruff voice shouted: 'They've gone into the maze! They've sunk themselves—they'll never get out of there! They'll get lost!'

Roberta felt around the bottom of the hedge, discovered that there was a good measure of clearance between the bottom of the trimmed privet and the ground and she rolled under the hedge where there was a winter-damp smell of earthiness. No sooner had she secured a place there than the path began to shudder to the thumping of heavy boots and she and Dacers, who was similarly sprawled out under the opposite hedge, were aware of boots rushing past them, their owners all unknowing that the two were within inches of their feet.

She saw, now, the cunning of Dacers' strategy. Cremorne, was obviously equipped with a maze, a plot of tantalizingly laid-out, neatly trimmed hedges in which visitors enjoyed getting lost until a man towering over them in a high chair pointed the way out when they became frustrated. Not functioning for the winter, its entrance was unsecured. Dacers had spotted it and caused the pursuing party to run into the heart of the puzzle.

She heard him stir from the hedge opposite and call her urgently: 'Come on, let's get out of here the way we came in. That crew are just about to discover they're the ones who've sunk themselves.'

The brief break gave the two a chance to recover their breath. They scrambled up and walked back towards the beginning of the path. Just as they reached it, an agonised yell came out of the depth of the maze behind them.

'Hey, Harry, Will—where are you? I took a wrong turning. I'm lost!'

An Americanised, equally agonised answer came: 'This is Will. I don't know where I am. I can't find Harry and the others and that blamed couple have plumb disappeared.'

Another voice wailed; 'I'm lost too, and I can't see a thing. Light a lucifer, somebody.'

Dacers and Roberta were now out in the open with the Big Tea Room shining like a beacon in the distance and startling them by showing them the long distance they had covered with their run. From the maze came an increased clamour from the lost men, now growing frustrated and profane. All was quiet in the gardens now and there was no sign of anyone from the disrupted meeting looking for satisfaction for the disturbance of their business. Dacers was sure he saw the man who had been addressing the meeting and the one similarly garbed in the group of runners who chased Roberta and himself so the meeting must have come to a total halt.

He led Roberta down a side path at the end of which a high wall could be dimly discerned.

'I hope you can climb that wall, Miss Van Trask,' said Dacers. 'It's our quickest way out. The Kings Road, Chelsea, lies on the other side. I hope you'll forgive me for remarking that your costume makes you look like an advertisement for a Christmas pantomime.'

She sniffed, 'Well, I think it turned me into quite a respectable young man. I came by cab and I did not seem to cause a sensation by appearing in public.'

'Then there must be more near-sightedness in London than I ever imagined,' he said wickedly. 'And that hat you're almost managing to keep on your head must be one of your father's I suppose.'

'It is and it's too big. I packed it with newspaper and all was well until I bumped into that iron tree thing I was hiding behind, I almost knocked my hat off, caused the tree to crash and gave everyone a chance to see I wasn't a male.'

Dacers laughed, remembering the comic figure she presented, running along in clothing too big for her, trying to hold her outsize hat on her head.

'To mention the unmentionable, are you wearing trousers?' he asked.

'Trousers of a kind. You must remember Mrs. Bloomer's dress reform for ladies. It became a positive mania when she introduced the idea to America before our big war.'

'It caught on here with radical ladies for a little time,' he said. 'Surely, you were only a youngster at that time.'

'Yes, a headstrong young schoolgirl. Our mothers disapproved of course, but we all tried the Bloomer costume on the sly. The Turkish trousers and the short skirt were very comfortable. I still have a pair of the trousers which I altered for tonight's venture. You don't know how daring and adventurous the American schoolgirl is.'

'I think I have good cause to know that some remain daring and adventurous after they cease to be schoolgirls,' commented Dacers.

They reached the wall which looked dauntingly high now they were close to it and Dacers' anxieties rose in case the men lost in the maze found the way out and came on their heels again. He stepped close to the wall and bent down, bracing himself with his hands on his knees.

'Climb on my back, jump up and you should be able to grip the top of the wall and haul yourself up. Sit up there and you can give me a hand up,' he told the girl. She responded quickly, climbing on his back, launching herself upward, clutching the top of the wall at the first attempt and reaching its flat top by pulling and scrabbling with her feet against the brickwork.

Sitting on the top, she reached down, gripped one of his hands and hauled him up with all her strength until he could throw his free hand up to grip the top bricks and take the strain from her arm by making an all-out effort to pull himself up. From their position on top of the wall they could see two ways along the King's Road with its twin rows of yellow street lights dimmed by the rags of wintery fog gathering about them. The road, normally busy, looked deserted. Dacers knew that their best chance of returning to town lay in catching a late-plying hansom cab if one could be found.

Descending from the top of the wall was easier than ascending it. They simply hung on to the top course of bricks by their fingers and dropped into the King's Road, still deserted of humanity and traffic. Now that he had gathered a normal rate of breathing, Dacers wanted to know why Roberta was eavesdropping on the meeting of the LUB, although he believed he already knew.

'When I last saw you, you were full of pious resolutions about taking up romantic novels and needlework to save your father from the anxiety your so-called detective antics might bring on,' he said. 'Yet, only a matter of hours later, here you are in a ridiculous disguise having been scared out of your hiding place and chased all over Cremorne Gardens. I don't know what that bunch would have done to you if they caught you.'

She looked at him like a penitent child, just caught out at some mischief and Dacers had to supress a sympathetic laugh at the sight.

'I gave in to my detective instincts', she Stated with grave dignity. 'I simply had to know what was going to happen at that meeting. I don't regret anything I did for a minute.'

'Yet you gained nothing but the benefit of a strenuous run. All I heard from the fellow doing all the talking was a history of the relationship between the State of Georgia and Great Britain. It meant nothing to me' Dacers said.

'That's because you came late. I learned a great deal before you arrived. These people and the movement they represent have quite astonishing plans of a kind that leave me in a quandary as to whether I should laugh or cry', she said. 'I was right in my guess at the name of their organisation. It is the League of the Unconquered Banner, taking up the spirit of Father Ryan's poem. So that should show you how uncannily gifted I am at solving a riddle.'

'Ah,' he breathed. 'So it is, as I thought, another group with foolish dreams of starting the war between the States all over again.' He was feeling irked, as when Roberta scored off him in their breakfast arguments. He was amused at her grotesque disguise and her dramatic notion of detective procedure but her foray into Cremorne Gardens against his express wish had obviously borne fruit.

'Tell me more,' said Dacers.

'No, later. Here comes a cab.'

The clop of hooves and the jingle of harness trappings came out of the thin mist cloaking the King's Road and the shape of the vehicle formed itself out of the murk. Dacers looked at Roberta and saw that a full-frontal view showed her to be wholly feminine.

'Quick' he said. 'Face me, put your arms around my neck and hang on. In that outfit, you still look like a girl and the cabbie could think you're in disguise and we're eloping—strange things happen in the vicinity of Cremorne. Keep your face hidden in the front of my coat and play my drunken young brother—but don't speak.'

The cab drew nearer.

'Cab!' shouted Dacers.

The vehicle halted and, from his high seat, the cabbie, wrapped around in the cabman's usual winter multiplicity of mufflers with his head haloed by pipesmoke, watched going on before his eyes a perfect rendition of a stock situation of the *Punch* cartoonists: a man trying to get his inebriated companion home.

With her arms around Dacer's neck and her tilted top hat kept turned away from the cabbie, Roberta allowed Dacers to more or less drag her to the cab. He opened the door and pushed her inside the vehicle before the cabbie had a chance to disengage himself from his seat and perform the cabbie's usual duty of helping his fares into his "London gondola".

CHAPTER 9

A DILEMMA FOR ROBERTA

''Ere, 'e ain't goin' to heave up in my keb, is 'e?' called the cabbie as Dacers settled Roberta into the limited space of the hansom's interior.

Dacers snorted and strode to the rear of the vehicle where the driver was perched on his seat near the roof.

'My good fellow, if you are insinuating that my brother can't hold his liquor, let me tell you that he could drink you and a full regiment of cabbies under the table any day you care to take up the challenge,' he called in the stentorian tones of the officer class. 'Furthermore, he's shown how well he can hold his drink in the company of some of the most eminent crowned heads in Europe including that of a most gracious and noble lady whose name I decline to bandy about in the vulgar surroundings of the street,'

''Ere, I didn't mean no offence, sir', said the cabbie, obviously affected by the suggestion of these fares having some royal connection. 'It 'as 'appened, y'know when gents 'ave been on the spree at Cremorne.'

'Such gents were no part of our clan,' Dacers retorted. 'Take us to Doric Square near Grosvenor Square and let us have no more jaw from you.'

He strode to the front of the cab again and climbed in to share the double seat with Roberta, chuckling.

'You can take the cabbie's remark as a comment on the excellence of your drunk act', he said.

He could see that she had learned through her eavesdropping—something that had profoundly affected her. As the hansom moved off, he asked: 'What did you hear at the meeting?

What was it that made you so undecided as to whether you should laugh or cry?'

'Their plans. They've got a completely crazy notion for the future of the State of Georgia that is so bold, I almost applaud it and wish it would succeed and, at the same time, I know it couldn't possibly work. I can see as plain as day it could easily set off a war between Great Britain and the United States. It's a desperate and dangerous reaction of a brave people who are being ill-used but it could only end in more misery.'

Dacers was growing frustrated. 'What is it? What do they want to do?' he almost demanded.

'They want to secede.'

'What? But Georgia seceded with a dozen other States in 1861 and look where it got them: wholesale loss of its young men in battle and, in the end, even its boys and old men, too and heaven knows how many were wounded. And there was the destruction of property, including the burning of Atlanta and the ruin of the State's economy.'

'You don't understand,' she said. 'They don't mean secession as it was done last time. They mean to take Georgia out of the union of States on its own and have it go back to being a British colony.'

Dacers gave a low whistle. '*What?* So that's why that fellow was harping on the Englishmen who started the original colony and did great things for it in its first days.'

'Yes, and, since the British are so solidly opposed to slavery, he reminded his audience that Georgia did not start out as a slave State', she said. 'The 'peculiar institution', as they like to call slavery, came later. And he reminded them that neutral Britain was reasonable enough to turn a blind eye to a Georgian, Commander James Bulloch, when he built and converted ships in Liverpool to serve the Confederate side in the war. He could not say enough about the goodwill between Georgia and Britain.'

'But this idea of an American State reverting to its old status as a British colony must be unconstitutional,' Dacers said. 'If the British government helped to make it a reality, it would spark off a war with the United States as you fear. The American government would see it as treason.'

'Someone brought that up at the meeting before you arrived and that sergeant-major fellow claimed Britain would hold all the cards,' Roberta said. 'She already has a far stronger navy than the US whose navy, which is small anyway, is exhausted after the Civil War. The army, too, is cutting its numbers and many of the wartime volunteer regiments have stood down. As for anything being unconstitutional, I'm not sure what is constitutional any more. Can it be constitutional for the Federal government to put the sovereign States of the South under military law and deal out such punishment? Mr. Lincoln was overjoyed by the end of the war. He declared we are one people again and he would never have acted as Mr. Johnson and his friends have.'

The hansom cab was making good time, speeding towards central London and Dacers absently watched the dark landscape passing by. He was thinking of what they had learned during their hectic visit to Cremorne Gardens and he asked Roberta: 'Didn't some of the Southern generals go to Mexico to join the Emperor of the French in his invasion after the Confederacy collapsed?'

'Yes, some of the best who survived—Simon Bolivar Buckner, Jubal A. Early, Kirby Smith and others. It was a betrayal of their American republican heritage to side with a monarchist invader from an alien land and you know I mean no reflection on your own monarchy.'

'Well isn't this proposal by these Georgians the same thing on a bigger scale? Instead of just a few soldiers choosing another flag, a whole State choosing to switch allegiance to another nation because it has lost faith in its own still divided nation?' said Dacers.

'Yes and it can only be doomed,' she replied. 'For one thing, the idea will not have the support of the whole State. The Georgia that developed as a true American State after our War of Independence is the only Georgia a great many will accept. I believe in the Union and in what Mr. Lincoln hoped to achieve. This League of the Unconquered Banner with its title taken from Father Ryan and slogan taken from John Wilkes Booth's shout of defiance obviously wishes to keep the old Confederate spirit alive in its traditions even if it goes under the British flag. That's why I'm torn between laughter and tears. It's so crazy as to be laughable and yet it's audacious and, in its way brave, I have some admiration for it. I guess only Georgia Crackers could dream it up, but the bulk of their fellow Crackers will turn it down flat.'

Dacers fell silent for a moment then said: 'There was mention of a Mr. O but I don't know where he fits into the LUB's plans. I have an inkling I know of him from a long time ago. He sounds like a fellow who once figured in a legal case and was tied up with the artistic world.'

The street lights became brighter as the cab drew nearer central London. Presently, the small window in the roof opened and the upper part of the cabbie's face appeared in it.

'Nearly at Doric Square, gentlemen,' he stated.

Roberta was leaning against Dacers' shoulder with her hat tilted over her face.

'Tell him to stop just inside the mews, where it's really dark,' she whispered. 'I'll go into the house by the back way and through the kitchen.'

Dacers instructed the face peering through the roof-window in a loud voice.

When the window clicked shut, he said, surprised: 'You've done this sort of thing before, haven't you? Rolling home late at night and going in by the back doors, I mean?'

'Yes, of course. Father almost never requires the coach and Richard in the evenings and he's a predictable creature of habit. We always have a late supper together but until supper time, Father keeps to his room with any papers from the embassy he needs to deal with, then he reads the latest American newspapers and the latest English ones. So, Esther and I have often had a pleasant evening outing in the coach with Richard driving, then home to supper.'

'All without your father's knowledge, I'll wager.'

'How did you guess?'

'And to think your father believed you needed to know more of London! Every day, I learn more about American tomboys who never cease to be tomboys or at least about one of them. Aren't you putting Richard in danger of losing his place?'

'Oh, Father would never discharge Richard, he's too good at his job. And you know what a big man he is. Any ladies under Richard's protection are well and truly protected.'

Their destination came into view and the cabbie steered his cab into the wide mews area at the rear of the Doric Square houses, which was in deep shadow. At this late stage, Roberta remembered the League of the Unconquered Banner and its objectives. It had provided Dacers and herself with a hectic evening but it had slipped her memory chiefly because she thought its aims were so utterly far-fetched that they could not possibly work. Nevertheless, she realised that she had a duty to the United States and it would be proper to report what she knew to either her father or directly to Ambassador Charles Francis Adams.

The roof window creaked open again.

'Doric Square, gentlemen,' reported the cabbie.

'What about the Georgia people who are here, trying to work mischief?' asked Roberta. 'Should I tell Mr. Adams or Father about them?'

Dacers's brain had been racing on that subject through the last part of the journey and, mingled with his concerns about it were those to do with the attempt on his life about which he had said nothing to Roberta for fear of frightening her. So far as he knew, the LUB had never heard of Septimus Dacers but was that body possibly working with anyone remaining of the Dixie Ghosts?

'No, give it twenty-four hours. I don't believe the Georgia people mean any harm—at least not in this country but there is another aspect to this affair I want to go into,' he told her.

Movements from the cabbie's high seat at the rear of the cab suggested the cabbie was coming down to assist his passengers in leaving the vehicle and Dacers did not want the man to discover that Roberta was neither a male nor intoxicated.

'I'll take care of things down here, cabbie, but wait awhile. I want you to take me to Bloomsbury.'

'Right y'are, sir,' answered the cabbie, probably grateful that he would be spared handling the hopelessly drunken young man he believed entered his vehicle.

Dacers opened the hansom's small, front-facing doors, helped Roberta out and went through the performance of assisting her drunken footsteps into the shadowy mews and up to the rear entrance to the house while she kept her face hidden.

Disgustedly, the cabman addressed his horse across the roof of the hansom: 'Blimey, Wellington, I thought me and my pals was uncommon good at soakin' up the grog when we were young 'uns but these toffs is a sight wuss than us—it's disgraceful!'

At the rear quarters of her home, Roberta said: 'I'm in good time to change for supper and Father won't even know I was out. He'll still be reading his papers in his room.'

Dacers considered her strange and slightly comic disguise.

'You're going through the kitchens dressed like that?' he asked.

'Yes, Cook and the domestics won't give me away. They're used to seeing me slip in the back way.'

Dacers shook his head as if in despair. 'What a simpleton I must be. Not so long ago, I thought you were the very essence of the sweet, innocent and gentle American rose.'

'Oh, come now, Mr. Dacers, you cannot have it both ways. You told me my pioneering spirit would always have me seeking what was on the other side of the hill,' she said with a laugh. 'I must say I am enjoying my first investigation, I realise we still have a lot to do.'

'We?' he echoed, 'Now, look here, young lady. I told you I would not take you on—' His protest died. 'Oh, forget it,' he said lamely.

He had told her he would not allow her to exercise her amateur detective talents in any of his investigations but this matter of the ambitions of the General from Georgia and his followers was not properly his investigation. It was something he was caught up in after Roberta drew his attention to the announcements appearing in the press.

She had every right to be concerned about the League of the Unconquered Banner. She was loyal to the United States, although not happy about the President's policies in the South. She was the daughter of a US diplomat and if the plans of the LUB amounted to a criminal or treasonable conspiracy against the United States, she had a right to be fully informed about it and to let her father and his chief, Charles Francis Adams, know about it.

Having reached this point in this intriguing affair Dacers had, in conscience to continue giving Roberta a helping hand. So they were jointly involved in the investigation, whether he liked it or not.

'Hurry inside before your father misses you. I do not know what advice to give you about this LUB matter, but it could plainly cause a serious diplomatic incident between Britain and the United States. It seems to me you must tell your father and Mr. Adams about it.'

'Leave all that to me. I've been thinking about what must be done ever since I heard that fellow making his speech,' she said firmly and the lamplight revealed that the usual mischievous twinkle had left her eyes and there was a determined look on her face.

He hastened back to the cab feeling the weight of the revolver in his pocket banging against his hip. It reminded him of the menace that had shown up in his life just before the hectic adventure in Cremorne Gardens—the false bearded horseman with the lame foot who was out to kill him and whom he was sure was from the Dixie Ghosts.

As the cab hurried him to Bloomsbury, Roberta made her appearance in the quarters she and Esther shared at the top of the house much to the relief of Esther, who only knew the mystifying fact that Roberta had disguised herself to go to Cremorne Gardens but was unaware of the reasons why.

'Well, here you are at last,' she said. 'It's nearly supper time and I was worried that you'd come to some harm at that terrible

Cremorne place. And I was worried that Mr. Van Trask might come up here and find you gone—what could I possibly say to him?'

'Oh, Esther, you need not have worried. You know Father never comes up here until after supper to wish us good night. I was perfectly safe at Cremorne. I met Mr. Dacers there and we had a very interesting time,' Roberta said.

Esther raised her eyebrows. 'Mr. Dacers was there, was he? I can't think what he was doing in that dreadful place. Or you, for that matter and I shan't ask but if he has any care for you, I hope he got you out fast.'

'You can be sure we were there on quite proper business,' said Roberta. 'And he got me out very quickly.' She smiled and added: 'As for caring for me, I'm convinced he does. And it's a very special kind of care.'

Esther read a significant message in Roberta's smile and her eyebrows shot up again.

CHAPTER 10

NEWS OF MR. O

By the time they escaped from the infuriating pattern of paths and hedges that made up Cremorne's maze, Lewis Sadler and Jefferson Dobbs were both in a towering rage. They had endured chilly hours of frustration with the rest of the party who thought they had chased the oddly dressed girl and the tall man with the long black sidewhiskers deep into the maze. They found themselves trapped in a black labyrinth while the fugitive pair had disappeared into thin air.

Their blunderings caused individuals to be lost in different parts of the maze but much hoarse calling and the use of many lucifer matches, finally resulted in the whole party gathering in one section then, by holding hands and moving through the darkness in a chain, they managed to come upon the way out.

The worrying disruption of the LUB meeting had ruined its whole purpose which was to encourage the supporters to spread throughout all the British Isles enthusiasm for the objective of replanting the flag of Great Britain on the State of Georgia. Hopefully, they would create a strong lobby to urge Parliament and influential trade and other bodies in what was developing into the British Empire to promote that end. With the meeting wrecked, Sadler and Dobbs had no opportunity to follow their agenda through. At this late hour, the participants in the meeting had gone home or, in the case of those who came from outside London, returned to their accommodation. The fiasco caused by the oddly disguised girl eavesdropper caused the audience to disperse, disappointed and grumbling.

It was dark, starless night by the time the escape from the maze was made. Almost all the attractions of Cremorne Gardens had closed down, though the gates had not yet closed and a few aimless souls, mostly intoxicated, wandered about the multiple paths.

The two men from Georgia, both glowering in silence, tramped one of the paths, looking for the way out of the gardens, when a small figure shambled towards them.

He stood in their path to halt them and the uncertain light from the few Chinese lanterns still burning showed a shabbily dressed little man with long, unkempt hair and a foxy face adorned by a straggling moustache.

'I've been lookin' for you gents. I was passin' that party you was givin' an' I 'eard you say you wanted to find Mr. O,' he said in a whining voice. 'Well, I can tell you where you can find 'im—for a consideration.'

This was good news indeed for Sadler and Dobbs and it dispelled their gloom after the experience of the maze and the collapse of their vital meeting. Unless, of course, this unprepossessing specimen of humanity was yet another of the great tribe of ragged scroungers with which London seemed to be overpopulated.

'A consideration?' said Sadler.

'Yus, you know—tin—gelt—money!'

'Oh, you'll get money when we get the information.'

'Done! But don't let 'im know it was me what gave you the office.'

'What do you mean, 'the office?' asked Sadler, uncertain of the Cockney argot.

'I figure he means it was him who told us where we can find O,' Dobbs said.

'How can we? We don't know his name,' Sadler said.

Their informant beamed. 'That's right. An' I ain't givin' it. Mr. O can turn nasty an' I don't want to cop a packet from 'im, that I don't. 'E lives in Putney. I dunno where but he takes 'is lunch in the Silver Moon chop house at about twelve-thirty every day.'

Where's Putney?' asked Lewis Sadler.'

'And where's the Silver Moon chop house?' asked Jefferson Dobbs.

'Putney's near 'ere, 'ard by the river and the Silver Moon is in Putney, on the road opposite the river, close to Putney Bridge and the big church' said their informant.

Sadler suddenly grabbed the little man by his skinny neck and pressed his Adam's apple with both thumbs.

'Now, give me your name and quick,' he demanded. 'You surely didn't think we would let you remain anonymous when you might have served up a pack of lies, did you? Name, quick, or you'll be throttled colder than a Thanksgiving turkey.'

''Arry Squibb an' I ain't told any lies.' The man gurgled. He was shivering like a leaf.

'And where do you live? If you've put us on a false trail, we'll come after you, hotfoot.'

'In a doss 'ouse in Thames Alley, Putney an' I ain't lied. I knows Mr. O takes 'is lunch at the Silver Moon because I works as part time potman there an' 'e's well known there. 'E'll be there tomorrow lunch time.'

Sadler released his grasp on the man's neck and Harry Squibb quickly regained his dignity—and his eye to the main chance.

'What about my consideration?' he asked.

Sadler shoved his hand into the pocket of his long topcoat, found a handful of coins, pulled them out and handed them to Squibb. He was still not fully acquainted with the values of the bewildering variety of English coinage: the sovereigns, half-sovereigns, half-crowns, florins, so he did not know how much he handed over.

Squibb scooted off into the darkness and under one of the last Chinese lanterns still burning, he examined his haul of cash then spluttered a string of invective against those he called 'bloody Yankees.' There was not a single gold half-sovereign among a clutch of lowly copper and silver coinage.

Harry Squibb had an exaggerated notion of American life and he marvelled at how tight-fisted the Americans could be when they lived in a land where money grew on trees and when there was a poor crop, one could always go to the goldfields and dig up a supply of precious metal.

Squibb gave a disgusted snort. 'Blimey,' he growled. 'I gave them coves valuable information an' got damn all in return. If I ever bumps into 'em again, they'll get nothing more out of me!

The following morning, in invigorating winter sunshine, Lewis Sadler and Jefferson Dobbs walked through Putney, having arrived by the suburban railway, one of the newer innovations now linking the capital's scattered outlying centres of settlement.

Putney in 1867 had a pleasing aspect. It was rapidly becoming a desirable middle-class riverside suburb with well-appointed new houses being built for those who had the wherewithal to settle into comfortable lives. The River Thames here had none of the smoke, squalor and din it had in the deeps of London where it became the mast- crowded 'Pool of London', the throbbing heart of the capital's shipping industry.

Along the river banks of Putney the only vessels to be seen were the those of a recreational nature, the bulk of them now sheeted in canvas and laid up for the winter. Their presence was testimony to Putney's gentlemanly interest in spare-time yachting and boating.

Lewis Sadler and Jefferson Dobbs walked along the road flanking the river, having been put on the right path for the Silver Moon Chop House by a man passing by. Behind them lay the almost unbelievably rickety wooden structure of Putney Bridge, linking Putney with Fulham across the river. Over the years, this venerable bridge was patched and re-patched until its dangerous condition caused constant public agitation. Just opposite the bridge rose the tower of the old parish church of St Mary and Putney High Street opened just beyond the church.

It was a little after noon on the day following the rumpus at Cremorne Gardens and Sadler and Dobbs hoped to target Mr. O when he visited the Silver Moon for lunch. They found the chop house facing the river, a building not greatly differing from the average pub in appearance. It was fronted by a small garden, planted with winter-bare shrubs and an old oak.

Only a short time before the arrival of the two Georgians, Mr. O had stepped into the dining room of the Silver Moon with his usual self-assured and cocky walk. He had recently settled in Putney and, after his summer wedding, intended to make the home of his wife and himself there. He had become known to many of the regular customers of the Silver Moon, for the most part, representatives of the middle-class businessmen and traders domiciled in Putney and a number of them uttered a greeting or nodded an acknowledgment when he entered.

The designation 'chop house' characterised the Silver Moon as male territory. Ladies were excluded. The air was filled with the burr of male conversation, cigar and pipe-smoke and the aroma of wines and spirits. The regulars at the Silver Moon fully fitted its atmosphere. They were most middle-aged with elegant whiskers and well-fed paunches on which gold watch chains bounced. O presented a hail-fellow-well-met façade towards them but he secretly despised their smug complacency. Any one of them might easily be courted by some skilful flattery until he fell for a well organised confidence trick. O thought that, some day, he might try it.

There were a few diners at tables set for meals in the room and O sat down at one of the empty tables, signalling with an amiable nod to Walter, the room's elderly, side-whiskered waiter. Walter shuffled over to the table and stood with stolid dignity at O's side.

'I'll take the today's ordinary with a glass of pale ale, if you please, Walter,' said O.

'As you please, sir,' droned Walter. The "ordinary" was every Victorian hostelry's substantial daily set meal, a favourite with the businessmen of the era and, when dining at the Silver Moon, O desired to fit convincingly into the part of a busy man of affairs.

It was just at that point, that the part-time potman, Harry Squibb, with his tattered clothing covered by a long, off-white apron, chose to emerge from the kitchen where his duties of washing pots and pans lay. The kitchen's doorway stood to one side of the main entrance of the Silver Moon and Squibb's path almost brought him into collision with two lean men just entering the hostelry. They were tall and wore long top-coats and broad-brimmed hats. They were the pair from America whom Harry Squibb encountered at Cremorne Gardens the night before.

Sadler and Dobbs were looking for positive results from their efforts on this side of the Atlantic. So far, everything had gone wrong and they hardly knew how they could ever face the General, back at home. The Birkenhead box had been stolen; Ned Grandon had unaccountably absconded, taking some of their allowance of money with him and the important meeting at Cremorne to rally the General's supporters to his cause had become a complete fiasco, thanks to some madcap girl disguised as a male. At last, they were within handling distance of the mysterious Mr. O who had knowledge of the box and they intended to handle him without kid gloves.

The aggressive glares of the pair almost froze the blood in Harry Squibb's veins. Lewis Sadler grinned humourlessly.

'Well, now here's a stroke of luck. We were just about to seek you out, my friend. Can you tell us if Mr. O has arrived for his lunch?' he asked.

Harry Squibb had vowed he'd never give information to these two ever again but their unfriendly scowls caused that resolution to melt away as an icy shiver slithered down his spine.

'Yes, he went into the dining room not two minutes ago,' said Squibb in a wavering voice.

'Good. Then be kind enough to point him out to us from the door of the dining room,' said Sadler. The men from Georgia were escorted to the dining room door by Squibb.

'That's him—the man sitting alone at that table,' Stated Squibb.

'Much obliged—now scoot!' said Sadler harshly but Squibb, evidently curious as to what the two Georgians intended to do to O, persisted in hanging around the dining room door.

'What're you waiting for? Some more of what you call a 'consideration'?' Jefferson Dobbs demanded, 'There's nothing coming to you—so scoot!'

Harry Squibb scooted back to the kitchen while Sadler and Dobbs walked directly to O's table. They stood, one on either side of his chair.

O looked from one man to the other, totally bewildered. He suddenly felt four large hands grab him, one pair under each armpit and could only utter an incoherent gurgle as he was hoisted bodily off the chair.

The patrons of the Silver Moon looked on aghast as the Georgians hauled O from behind the table then frogmarched him towards the door.

One screwed his eyeglass into his eye and surveyed the re-treating backs of the three.

'I say, I was always suspicious of that chap', he commented to a crony. 'Who do you suppose the pair in the long coats are?'

'Bailiffs, plain as day!' grunted the crony. 'The fellow obviously owes money. I knew all along the blighter was a bad lot. Not our kind of chap at all!'

O was unwilling to go without a struggle as Sadler and Dobbs bore him out of the chop house door. He wriggled and struggled in vain efforts to free himself but the two Georgians held him securely and dragged him along between them when he declined to co-operate and walk.

Outside, he was dumped like a sack of wet sand behind a shrub in the garden fronting the Silver Moon. With winter still in the air, the shrub was bereft of foliage but it still masked what might go on behind it from passers-by in the street.

O made a struggling, panting effort to rise but Sadler and Dobbs pounced on him and held him down with their combined weight, forcing him against the hard wintery earth.

'Who are you and what d'you want?' O managed to gasp.

'A couple of gentlemen from far away and we want the long box you had a hand in stealing from Birkenhead', Sadler Stated flatly.

'Don't know what you're talking about,' O responded stubbornly though he felt an uncomfortable chill surging through his being.

Sadler was holding his legs down and Dobbs was sitting on his chest. Dobbs pushed his hand into a pocket of his topcoat and brought out a Colt revolver. He held it before O's white face and cocked it. Dobbs then took hold of O's nose and squeezed it hard. This caused O to open his mouth wide. Dobbs pushed the barrel of his pistol into his mouth and held it hard against the roof of his mouth.

'Better talk fast,' advised Dobbs. 'Talk fast because this gun and I mean business, bub. Where is that box?'

Dobbs glowered dangerously into O's ashen face. 'C'mon, let's have the answer before I lose my patience and put a bullet up into your brain,' he demanded.

He took the pistol out of O's mouth. O made a series of choking, gagging noises and tried to find his voice. He was thoroughly unnerved by the feel of the hard barrel of the Colt against the roof of his mouth.

Dry-mouthed, he managed to say: 'In a place near Southampton Row, in the middle of London.'

'We want more than that,' Sadler cut in threateningly. 'We want the proper address. C'mon, let's have it.'

'Marlborough Dwellings,' gabbled O. 'In Thistle Street. Number Two Marlborough Dwellings. I left it with a young fellow named Adolphus Crayford.'

'How do we know that's not just a pack of lies?' persisted Lewis Sadler.

'It's the truth,' said O. 'Honest, it's the absolute truth!'

O had been in tight spots before in his life but never in one so tight as this and he had never encountered men so ruthlessly determined as this pair. He guessed they had been moulded by the recent American war and the extraordinary savagery of that conflict had imprinted its brutal mark upon them. When they threatened violence they did so in a way which seemed to guarantee they were not uttering idle threats.

O fought for breath and knew he had to get out of this situation before he stopped a bullet.

Sadler had relaxed his hold on O's legs slightly. O wriggled his feet and found them fairly free. He planted them on the ground. Fear and desperation gave him the strength to jerk his legs upward, shaking off Sadler's hands.

His arms were free and he managed to plant his hands against the ground and made a near supernormal effort to push his whole body off the ground and dislodge Jefferson Dobbs from his chest, not caring that Dobbs' pistol might go of accidentally. Dobbs fell over to one side and sprawled in the sparse grass, losing his grip on his pistol. Sadler made an attempt to regain a grip in the lower part of O's legs again but O kicked his hands away.

Almost before he realised it and not knowing where he found the energy, O was uncurling himself from the ground and staggering to his feet. He started to run in blind panic for the roadway opposite the Silver Moon.

Rolling on the ground, Dobbs gathered up his Colt and, spluttering and swearing, and, in his typically impetuous way, levelled it at O's retreating back.

Sadler barked a hoarse objection: '*No!* This whole country is in a fever, terrified of the Irish Fenians starting a shooting campaign, A shot will bring every policeman for miles around! Get after him, quick!'

The two Georgians ran out of the Silver Moon's small garden and saw O running along the road ahead of them in the direction of Putney Bridge and the church. Both attempted to put on speed but the effort bore upon them the truth that they were no longer the lithe young men they once were and, since both were in the the flat-out pursuit of Dacers and Roberta Van Trask in Cremorne Gardens the previous evening, their reserves of stamina had not been replaced.

O put all his effort into his flight. He had no desire to fall into the hands of the dangerous pair of Americans again. The one with the revolver seemed to have a particular streak of viciousness and O had no wish to feel the threatening steel of his pistol rammed against the roof of his mouth again.

Even in the midst of his alarm, questions concerning the box from Birkenhead began to form in his brain. His earlier fear had been that the police would come in search of it, following up information from Birkenhead, due to the American exile who was robbed being a respected international celebrity. The two men on his tail had shown a desire to obtain the box so intense that they were prepared to resort to gunplay to obtain it. They were plainly no policemen but the box must contain something of peculiar value and, even in the heat of his flight, O saw that it would be better in his hands again rather than hidden away in the obscurity of Adolphus Crayford's tiny apartment. If he got out of his present predicament, he would take pains to retrieve it. It must be of greater value than he ever imagined and he was foolish to part with it in the first place.

But gasping breath, blood drumming at his eardrums and feet that were beginning to falter, forced recognition of the acuteness of his present predicament on him. He was growing weary. A needle-like stitch was beginning to stab at his side. As his lungs began to labour, he wondered if the scented Turkish cigarettes he virtually devoured were starting to tell on him.

He glanced over his shoulder but could not see his pursuers. Then he noted that he had turned a bend in the road and they were still behind it but would make their appearance at any moment. He forced as much speed as he could out of his unwilling legs. He was now running with Putney's winter-sheeted recreational craft on the river to his right while the old wooden bridge and St Mary's Church were looming ahead.

The churchyard was crammed with high grave stones and monuments behind its low stone wall. He ran for the wall, praying he would reach it before the pursuers rounded the bend. He succeeded and scrambled over the wall, feeling that his breath was about to give out. He saw a row of high, weather worn gravestones ahead of him and, ducking low, he flung himself down behind one, fighting to recover his breath. There was an unkempt mixture of long grass and weeds around the grave and this, as well as the gravestone, offered cover. He was well out of sight of the churchyard wall.

He waited, slowly recovering normal breathing and listening for any sound of the two Americans.

Eventually, from beyond the wall, he heard trudging feet and a wearied, laboriously panting American voice said: 'Damn it! I figure he came this way and he plumb disappeared. Reckon he's somewhere in this graveyard. Where's the gate to it. I'm too blamed tuckered out to climb this wall!'

'Back this way, near the main gate to the church, I guess,' gasped his companion, who was obviously just as winded.

O came to his knees, keeping his body almost doubled, he scooted back among the graves, crossing the churhyard until he reached the low wall flanking Putney High Street. Climbing the wall, he quickly plunged into the street's crowded mixture of humanity, horses and vehicles to become almost invisible and make a hasty, stumbling way back to the shelter of his lodgings.

There, he lay low for the rest of the day. He was a man with almost monumental nerve, a smooth-talking chancer, the very model of the 'chickaleery bloke' of the music hall song, who had carried out some audacious misdeeds in a reckless life, but terror now gripped him. The two determined Americans might still be prowling the streets of Putney, looking for him and he had no wish to feel the barrel of a cocked pistol rammed into his mouth again. It took a long time for him to gain something resembling his composure and his cocky sense of superiority again. He smoked a fistful of his scented Turkish cigarettes and littered the floor with their miniscule butts, as usual, smoked down to almost nothing.

O was scared but not scared enough to be to be wholly cured of the avarice that drove his criminality. If anything, his greed had been sharpened by his encounter with the pair from America,. He now knew that the box he once had in hands contained something so desirable it brought out murderous intentions in the two. They had terrorised him into divulging its whereabouts but he wanted to possess it and its obviously valuable contents once again.

He determined to hasten to Thistle Street and collect the box from Adolphus Crayford's keeping but he dare not venture out while there was a possibility of the men from America being somewhere in Putney scouring the streets for him with their murderous desire to obtain the box intensified by his escape.

He would have to wait until the following day before he attempted a return to young Crayford's lodging. He entertained the wild hope that the pair might have forgotten the young artist's address address since neither had noted it down but dismissed it, feeling the pair were probably too sharp and too intent on finding the box for that.

By tomorrow morning, the two Americans would surely have cleared out of Putney he would take the suburban train into London proper, hoping they had not beaten him to Marlborough Dwellings and seized the box. That object meant money and nothing lured O like money.

With hands still shaking, he lit another cigarette.

CHAPTER 11

CONSULTATION WITH A SAGE

Septimus Dacers made his way over the broken cobbles and between the dismal houses and tenement dwellings of Seven Dials, one of London's most deprived, depraved, villainous and starvation-haunted corners. "The Dials" ranked as a blot on the face of Queen Victoria's booming capital city. Its crumbling courts and unsavoury alleys sheltered a ragged population steeped in every species of trickery and criminality. It was a place to be avoided by any man with a pocket to be picked or a watch to be lifted. Worse, in dusk or darkness a shadow might slip behind him, swiftly snatch off his hat, bring a cosh down on his skull and rob him of everything on his person that could be stolen, including items of his clothing. No respectable woman would ever cross the margin separating Seven Dials from the well policed London of civilised behaviour.

And yet it was in Seven Dials that one of London's most enigmatic personalities, a veritable sage who seemed to know every heartbeat of the great city, chose to make his home. It was to visit him that Dacers was on his way It was the day after he and Roberta Van Trask were chased through Cremorne Gardens; the self-same day when the two Georgians and Mr. O clashed in Putney.

As he threaded his way through the unlovely cityscape of Seven Dials, several things were on Dacers'mind: the attempt to shoot him; the information gleaned from the meeting at Cremorne concerning the unbelievable plans to bring Georgia out of the United States and into the burgeoning British Empire and the reference to a certain 'Mr. O' which brought a vague memory out of the past.

He came to a tumbledown structure over whose door a battered board bore the information that this was the establishment of *Seth Wilkins, Practical Engraver.*

Setty Wilkins, small and gnome-like whose age none had ever guessed, the very Cockney of all Cockneys who spoke the Cockney argot that went out thirty years before, sat at his work desk, smoking his pipe and reading a book. When he heard the door creak open, he closed his book and pushed it to one side. It was *Lord Chesterfield's Letters to His Son.* There was far more to Seth Wilkins than met the eye.

When the tall form of Dacers stepped through the door, Setty gave a throaty chuckle.

'Vell, look vot's blown in from the great, salty sea,' he chortled. 'Mr. Dacers hisself, in the flesh and accept no substitoots. Votcher, Mr. Dacers?'

'Fine, thank you, Setty' said Dacers. 'How are you?'

'If lumbago, rheumatism and corns vos currency of the realm, I'd be rich as Rothschild but you vants to know somethin', Mr. Dacers. You're velcome as the flowers in May but every time you enters my place of creative endeavour, I catches on to you avantin' to know somethin.' Oh, I'm glad to see you all abubble with curiosity. It means you're in the course of earnin' a crust, vich is allus a healthy occupation.'

Dacers grinned and sat down on a wooden box, part of the general clutter that furnished Setty's workplace.

'What I want to know, Setty, is how you came to be a human cabinet of curiosities where knowledge of London is concerned. When I learn how Setty Wilkins knows what's going on and what's gone on all over the city—and even, it seems what's about to go on in the future—when nobody can recall him ever leaving the Dials I'll retire content knowing that I've solved the greatest mystery of the universe. A detective can ask for nothing more.'

Setty removed his pipe from his mouth and his wrinkled face split into a wide grin. He tapped the side of his nose with his forefinger, a gesture which in the shadowy quarters of the

Cockney world meant *"That's for me to know and you to find out"* among other things.

'Vy, Mr. Dacers, it's easy vhen you knows how,' he said jovially. 'I'll write the secret of it in my vill for you. Now, how can I help you in vot you are chasin' up at this moment?'

'Do you recall, Setty, some years ago there was a fellow whose name began with an O who was in the artistic swim in lots of ways. There was some legal row he was concerned which had to do with some supposedly ancient glasswork that turned out to be quite modern?'

Setty gave a sharp laugh. 'Oh, I knows the cove you means. Mr. O he's called in some quarters and Owl in some others. Rum kind of bloke, wery thick with the painting and poetry crowd, Rossetti, Burne-Jones, Vhistler and Svinburne, though I 'eard Burne-Jones considers 'im a rogue and Svinburne don't like 'im either. It ain't none of my business but vot do you vant to know about 'im?'

'All a matter of research, Setty. I'd like to know where he can be found. In fact, I'd like to meet him.'

'Vell, me vot's a religious man in my own vay can only put it down to the mysterious vorkings of Providence, but only wery recent, I had vord of that same Mr. O;' Setty said. ''E's a downy bird an' a slippery one. 'E's not the kind to stay in one place for too long but a young man vot comes in here regular vith plates for me to 'grave for the penny dreadfuls had some business vith him not long ago. He might know vhere he can be found. This young gent is an artist and a good 'un, a son of a man of the cloth who deserves to make good one day. He came in here only recent cock-a-'oop because he'd sold a set of paintings to Mr. O and said 'e got a good price. I warned him to guard 'is dealin's with the man because there's many a tale that 'e's responsible for a deal of trickery in the art vorld. He gave young Mr. Crayford vot Mr. Crayford considered a good price for his pictures but rumours say 'e's the kind of cove vot might 'ave a vay of sellin' 'em on for a much better price. I can't think Mr. Crayford really likes him. He told me Mr. O likes scented Turkish cigarettes vhich he smokes all the time, one arter the other stinkin' everywhere out. Smokes 'em in a rum vay, too, accordin' to Mr. Crayford. Sucks 'em dry so to speak and leaves almost nothin' to throw avay.'

'Mr. Crayford, is that the young man's name?'

'Yus, Mr. Adolphus Crayford. 'e never told me 'is full address, but I know it's somewhere Southampton Row vay.' Setty paused, scratched his bald dome then suddenly looked inspired. 'Just a moment, though, I think ve can find it.'

He left his seat, walked to the rickety door and opened it. He bellowed into the street: 'Melbourne! Melbourne! Vhere are you lurkin' you young wagabond?'

As if by magic, a grinning boy of about thirteen appeared on the doorstep. He wore tattered clothing, crushed old boots made for someone with bigger feet, an ancient top hat so misused as to resemble a concertina, and a ragged scarf long enough to threaten to trip him.

'I ain't far away, Mr. Wilkins,' he declared brightly. 'I never am, knowin' you might need me any minute.'

'Come in, you brigand,' Setty invited. 'This gentleman is Mr. Dacers. 'e comes 'ere once in a while to discuss confidential business—confidential, mind, so don't you ever say you've seen 'im 'ere.'

Melbourne tapped his nose in that familiar Cockney gesture and grinned at Dacers. A child of the Seven Dials, his father who had long ago abandoned his brood of youngsters, must have had that strange weakness of the British lower classes of loving a lord. Otherwise it was difficult to understand why the boy was christened with the title of a former aristocratic Prime Minister who despised the poor.

'Melbourne, didn't I vunce send you to find out vhere young Mr. Crayford lives to deliver a set of 'gravings to him because he couldn't collect 'em 'isself? If you remember the address, give it to Mr. Dacers.'

'Easy, Mr. Wilkins. It's in Marlborough Dwellin's in Thistle Street at the back of Southampton Row. It's a pad, up the first stair, second door and the number is two. I had to watch my step, askin' around to find the place. There was three of four crushers lurkin' around the vicinity. They'd arrest a cove like me in no time, claimin' I was out to crack a crib.'

'Vhich is somethin' I 'ope you never contemplate, 'avin' tried to get you to respect the Ten Commandments,' said Setty gravely, wagging a finger at Melbourne.

Dacers fumbled in his pocket and found a florin which he handed to the urchin.

'Thank you, Melbourne. It's a good thing you have such a sharp memory. You've done me a service,' he said.

The boy looked at the coin with delight in his eyes. 'Cor! Two whole bob! Thanks, Mr. Dacers, you're a real toff!' he exclaimed.

Setty fished in the pocket of his engraver's apron and brought forth a shilling which he handed to Melbourne whose eyes lit up even more brightly.

'My eye! Thanks, Mr. Wilkins—now it's three whole bob!' he enthused.

'Use it to get something at the cookshop for yourself and your brothers and sisters and don't let your ma get it so she can blow it on gin,' warned Setty.

'I shan't,' grinned Melbourne. 'D'you still want me, Mr. Wilkins?'

'No. Run off. I'll signal you vhen I vants you again.'

Melbourne left the premises and Setty Wilkins turned to Dacers. He nodded to the door which Melbourne had just slammed. 'That's a bright young shaver I 'opes to save from jail or the gallows if I can. A lad like 'im could easily become one of the Swell Mob an' that'd be 'is ruin.'

Dacers smiled. He always knew there were hidden depths to Setty Wilkins. The old engraver now and then revealed a measure of unexpected learning. Dacers had heard him quote, Shakespeare, Dr Johnson, Lord Chesterfield and poets as old as Andrew Marvell and as modern as Tennyson.

He recalled that, during the affair of the Dixie Ghosts, an unknown urchin, quite likely out of Seven Dials, ran into the Scotland Yard detective office to deliver a message beneficial to Dacers to his friend, Detective Inspector Amos Twells. He suspected that the boy and the message were sent by Setty. Indeed, he had a notion that Setty used a squad of tattered urchins to carry out all manner of chores and bring back all manner of gossip from all over the city with which he was so familiar without ever leaving "The Dials".

He believed, too, that Setty Wilkins was a generous benefactor of the ragged youngsters of Seven Dials. Once again, Dacers left Setty's premises indebted to the Sage of Seven Dials and thinking of the mysterious Mr. O whose whereabouts might be known to the young artist in Marlborough Dwellings, Thistle Street.

The old engraver had reminded him of this shadow from the past. For O had a way of remaining shadowy in his dealings and he kept himself shadowy, too. Dacers recalled hearing of him as a general factotum among the artists and writers but very little was known about him outside artistic circles. Typically, Dacers had all but forgotten him after he faded from the headlines following the affair of the spurious antique glass for O seemed to have a way of fading away. But he had been mentioned by the speaker at the Cremorne gathering. What had he in his possession wanted by the former soldiers of the South who came to England hawking the improbable dream of Georgia becoming a British colony again?

And did he have any connection with another man from the South, the false-bearded horseman who came within an ace of shooting Dacers?

Clearly, there was more than a hint of criminality about Mr. O and he might need careful handling if Dacers encountered him. Hopefully, Adolphus Crayford of Marlborough Dwellings could tell him where O might be found. But he would delay seeing young Crayford until the morning. Tonight, he desired to call on Miss Van Trask as a matter of urgency.

CHAPTER 12

THE GLOOM OF MR. GRANDON

Victorian etiquette dictated that a gentleman must adhere to certain rules of conduct when calling on a lady. So, on the evening of his visit to Setty Wilkins, Septimus Dacers presented himself on the doorstep of Theodore Van Trask's home, near Grosvenor Square in a slate-grey topcoat, gloves a well brushed top hat and carrying a stick.

He yanked the bell-pull which brought Frederick, the family's elderly, frozen faced butler, to the door.

'I'm calling on Miss Van Trask, Frederick, though I'm not expected,' Dacers said.

The ghost of a knowing smile flickered over Frederick's usually immobile face. 'I'm sure Miss Roberta is always at home to *you,* sir,' the butler said. 'Do step inside.'

Roberta met him in the small ante-room off the entrance hall. She wore an elegant crinoline of green velvet and seemed to be glowing with good spirits. Evidently the hectic experiences and the chase through Cremorne Gardens the previous evening had not put her out in the least.

'Miss Roberta, I wanted to smooth things out with you and acquaint you with a new development concerning the fellows at Cremorne last evening,' he said.

'Smooth things out?' she queried, frowning.

'Yes, The other day, when you showed such sharpness in seeing the connection between Father Ryan's poem and the newspaper messages to the LUB members, I said you might make a professor of literature but hardly a detective. That was ungracious of me. Your acute reasoning made you put your finger on this LUB affair being some form of American conspiracy and you deserve praise for it. Look at what we now know—an almost unbelievable plan to unhook Georgia from the rest of the American nation and even start hostilities between our two nations.'

Roberta gave a light laugh. 'Oh, my goodness, you had no need to be troubled. I took no offence.' Her eyes suddenly twinkled and he saw her old tomboy spirit in her face as she added, mischievously: 'After all, Mr. Dacers, you were simply acting true to form—merely being a natural man.'

She smiled at him disarmingly with her face lit up with what he hoped was affection and he felt a surge of undeniable love for her.

'You said there's a new development in what I am going to boldly call our case, she said. 'What is it?'

'You might recall that the American fellow who addressed the meeting at Cremorne spoke of someone called Mr. O who had something he and his friends want. It seemed to me that this man might be a key to finding out more about the antics of these fellows from Georgia if we could locate him. Well, I now know who he is—a man with a very murky background who figured in some devious work years ago. And I know of a man who might know his whereabouts. I hope to see him tomorrow morning and maybe he can lead me to Mr. O.'

'You mean lead *us* to Mr. O, do you not? Surely you now fully agree that we are sharing this case. I'd like to come with you to find this man who can lead us to this other man,' said Roberta. 'Is he in London?'

'Yes and not very far from Bloomsbury. He's a young artist living in Marlborough Dwellings in Thistle Street near Southampton Row. There's no need for you to come along. It's only a matter of seeking him out and talking to him.'

Roberta looked at him with her exaggerated pout. 'I'd like to go with you. I feel you have accepted me as a *bona fide* assistant and I'd like to follow up every move.'

'There's really no need for you to be involved with this aspect of the affair. I'll see what transpires after finding our artist and I'll keep you well informed' he said. Then he added gravely:

'There's something I have not told you. There are some aspects possibly arising out of this affair that are distinctly dangerous. Only a couple of days ago, a man tried to shoot me in the street.'

Roberta's mouth fell open with shock and she listened with wide eyes as he outlined the incident with the mounted gunman.

'I have his gun which he dropped,' he told her. 'It bears some reference to a Georgia regiment and you'll remember that the men in Cremorne Gardens were former Confederates from Georgia. I feel that the gunman was involved with them but, at the same time, I have an uncanny feeling he was somehow mixed up in that Dixie Ghosts matter. After all, I can't think the LUB people have any quarrel with me. It might be that the deeper we go into this affair, the more likely we are to encounter people who will shoot. And I will not put you at risk.'

Roberta gave him an enigmatic smile. 'My father firmly believes that I can never come to any harm when I'm with you,' she stated. 'So long as I was under your protection, I don't think he'd worry how many guns were ranged against us.'

He looked at her in near astonishment. 'Then he must have a remarkably high opinion of me,' he gasped.

'He has. And let me tell you of the new development I have to report. Last night I had a heart-to-heart talk with my father. I took your advice, realising that I should let both Mr. Adams and my father know about what we heard at Cremorne Gardens. After all, it's all very serious, verging on treason if not actually treasonable. My loyalty to the United States was challenged and I could not keep quiet about what I knew. I just had to tell him about how I went to Cremorne and what I heard and how we were chased. I kept nothing back. He was startled and very concerned by news of the Georgia plot but he praised what you did to get me out of the fix I put myself into. He even seemed proud of me and astonished me by laughing and saying he was pleased the old Van Trask adventurous spirit was still alive and said I should not go far wrong so long as I was with Septimus Dacers. Then he had me write out all I heard at Cremorne Gardens to pass on to Mr. Adams who'll have to report the matter to Washington.'

Dacers gave a low whistle of surprise. 'It looks as if we've sparked off an urgent international incident,' he commented. 'We disrupted the meeting our friends from Georgia organised to whip up support for their plans. They'll possibly never reconvene it if the chiefs in Washington and London get their heads together and act quickly to jointly scotch the LUB's plans. Meantime, though, I still intend to follow up the attempt on my life and chase Mr. O and whatever it is he owns that is so important to the men from Georgia. I'll still call on young Mr. Crayford in Thistle Street early tomorrow.'

Roberta put on her mock pout to look like a disappointed child.

'And I still wish I was coming with you,' she said.

The morrow brought a morning of sharp frost coupled with stimulating sunshine. It was the sort of day to inspire men to action and five men in different parts of London set out to journey to a single destination. The destination was Marlborough Dwellngs, in Thistle Street, Three of the men sought possession of the long wooden box, stolen from the Birkenhead home of a distinguished American exile.

The third man was Septimus Dacers who wanted to meet Adolphus Crayford and discover the whereabouts of Mr. O.

The fifth man embarked on a journey that morning with a different object in view and finished up heading to Marlborough Dwellings against his will. He was Ned Grandon who met the morning in a sweat of apprehension and a state of near panic he could scarcely control.

The earliest abroad was Mr. O. He left his Putney lodging when it was barely daylight to take the first suburban train into awakening London proper. He hurried to the station still fearful that the pair from America might still be lurking in Putney's streets and could jump on him with bloodthirsty intent from any shadowy corner.

Septimus Dacers was out of doors considerably later. His path to Thistle Street was much shorter. He needed to navigate a few of Bloomsbury's streets and cross the pleasant expanse of the gardens in the middle of Russell Square to reach Southampton Row.

Not far away, in Camden Town, Lewis Sadler and Jefferson Dobbs were setting out from their lodging at the home of the supplier of breech-loading rifles to the Confederate States whom they hoped would support Georgia's breakaway plans with money. They had very definite ideas about obtaining the box General Edmund Vavasour required so urgently. The terrified O had revealed that a certain man named Crayford had it in his keeping at Thistle Street. If Crayford proved reluctant to hand it over, some of the rough play learned in the American Civil War would come into play and he would be forced to hand it over. The carefully laid plan to organise the League of the Unconquered Banner among Georgia's friends in Britain at the Cremorne Gardens meeting had been thrown into chaos thanks to the interference of the ludicrously disguised unknown girl and her equally unknown male companion.

The Georgian General's agents, however, now had a definite lead to the box stolen from Birkenhead and, by hook or by crook, Sadler and Dobbs were determined to collect it. Possession of it would give them at least one face-saving triumph when they reported back to Vavasour in Georgia.

Then there was the fifth man, Ned Grandon. The world of the mid-Nineteenth Century did not know the word neurosis, but Grandon was very firmly in the grip of a neurosis that numbed his brain and almost paralysed his thought. He was decamping from the home of his relatives in Somers Town, leaving bag and baggage behind. He had run so low on cash that after handing over a few pounds to placate his cousin's dunning for rent he was nearly penniless.

Not for the first time, he wondered if the mental strain and ill-usage he had suffered during the American war had thrown his brain out of kilter. His obsession with killing Septimus Dacers to avenge his criminal brother caused him to dream up an elaborate plan which ended in disaster. He had become prey to nagging terrors of persecution. He felt the police might seize him at any moment for his attempt to shoot Dacers. He was haunted by the illogical fear that the livery stable owner was close on his tail, demanding satisfaction for the horse swept away in the ride of panicking cattle with the muscles of prize-fighter friends to back his claim.

In his fevered imagination, he was a wanted man, stranded in London without money and he did not leave his cousin's household entirely because of rent. He did not want Hector and his family lifted by the police if they tracked him down for the murder attempt.

Like Sadler and Dobbs, Grandon was to have stayed with the London friend of the old Confederacy the maker of breech-loading rifles and a supporter of General Vavasour's plot to turn back the clock in Georgia. He knew the man's Camden Town address and set out for it that morning. Long before embarking for Liverpool, he made up his mind to abscond to London and put up at his cousin's home to follow his own mission to avenge the imprisoning of his brother, Howard and the ruination of the Dixie Ghosts.

Now, with the bleak feeling that his plans were totally wrecked, it seemed his only course of salvation was to reconnect with his two companions from Georgia. They had money and could obtain more from LUB contacts in England. They could ensure his ultimate return to America.

They would see his desertion as treason and, doubtless, both would want to shoot him the moment they set eyes on him but he'd spin a yarn of running off to London in a hurry because of some crisis among his relatives there. He'd wheedle his way into their acceptance once more and he'd eat humble pie with grovelling assurances that he had not deserved General Vavasour or the aims of the LUB.

He'd remind them that he was still their comrade in arms, a proud veteran of the regiment called Vavasour's Georgia Crackers who had shared their battlefield hardships and had suffered for the old flag.

He made his limping way into Camden Town trying to instil some confidence into his queasy innards by rehearsing what he would say to Sadler and Dobbs. Their lodging was in

Mornington Street and he was just turning into that thorough-fare when he saw both men walking toward him.

He was spotted first by Jefferson Dobbs who gave an almost choking splutter of surprise then a growl of anger.

'I can't believe what I'm seeing!' he exclaimed. 'Look who's coming along the street and heading straight for us—Ned Grandon! The double-dyed, treacherous polecat who ran out on us is showing up bold as brass. By God, I'll put a bullet in him!' He moved his hand impetuously towards his coat pocket but Sadler grabbed his arm.

'Wait!' he commanded. 'I'm as mad at him as you but leave him be! Let's find out where he's been and what he's been up to and what's happened to the money he ran off with.'

The two hastened their footsteps to meet up with Grandon.

'Explain yourself!' barked Sadler when they were face to face.

'Yes, explain yourself pronto or it's a bullet for you,' snarled Dobbs with his hand in his topcoat pocket.

'Well, I'm sorry I ran out on you but, before leaving the States, I had word that things were not well with my London relatives and they needed help. I didn't mention it at the time but, when we reached Liverpool, I got a big notion to run off to London as quick as possible.' He delivered his excuse in a voice nearly as thin as the excuse itself.

Lewis Sadler glowered into his face. 'See here, Grandon, you have more explaining than that to do and you'll be made to. It happens that we know where that box from Birkenhead is and we're off to collect it. You'll not be let out of our sight and you're coming with us.'

'And I'll be behind you every step of the way—with a loaded Colt in my pocket!' promised Jefferson Dobbs.

CHAPTER 13

CONTEST FOR THE BOX

Mr. O, whom some called 'Owl', was the first of the men bound for Marlborough Dwellings to arrive there. It was still early and the unpretentious street was empty. Its residents were of the poorer classes who, if they had any occupation at all, had usually to be out extraordinarily early to fulfil long hours.

O was still fearful of an encounter with the pair from America and could not help worrying that that they might even have reached Thistle Street the night before after leaving Putney. He pinned all his hopes on being the first on the scene in Thistle Street that morning and, if his luck was in, he would collect the box from young Crayford and bear it away without mishap. At the woebegone frontage of Marlborough Dwellings, with one of his Turkish cigarettes jutting from his mouth, he hastened into the doorless entrance and climbed the creaking stairs to Adolphus Crayford's small apartment. He knocked on the door but received no answer. He knocked again with the same result. Thinking Crayford might still be in bed, he called his name but there was still no answer.

Could it be that young Crayford had stepped out for a brief time, perhaps to one of the shops in Southampton Row to make a purchase? He decided to descend to the front of the building to perhaps catch Crayford returning. He did so, looked up and down the empty street and stood for a time, smoking furiously until his cigarette was the smallest of butts. This he tossed away and immediately lit up a fresh cigarette. He had hardly begun to smoke it when he was aware that time was wasting and he must do something about obtaining the box immediately. He threw away the new cigarette impatiently, quickly entered the tenement building and climbed the stairs again.

At the door of Crayford's room, he turned the knob and pressed the door inwards. Everything in this building was old and sub-standard and the lock was obviously not strong, Some pressure on the door with a man's shoulder would surely cause the lock to yield. O placed his shoulder against the door and forced the wood inward. He did not need to charge the door and thus alert others living along the corridor. The door creaked and the lock yielded. The door swung inward and fell slanting on its hinges. With desperate eagerness, O stepped into the young artist's apartment.

He made a bee-line for the corner where he had deposited the box and with a sense of relief quivering through his whole body saw it was still there. He grasped it and hastily made for the door again.

Outside, Septimus Dacers arrived in Thistle Street, finding it empty except for a scraggy, villainous looking cat. He saw the ugly bulk of the tenement building and read its title formed in moulded lettering over the entrance. As he approached the doorway, he was aware of a sweet aroma in the air—that of Turkish cigarettes. He looked on the ground and saw a butt, smoked to almost nothing and not far from it a fuller cigarette, still alight and sending up a thin ribbon of aromatic smoke.

He recalled what Setty Wilkins had told him of O's smoking habit: how he smoked Turkish cigarettes until there was almost nothing left of them. Mr. O, the man of dubious character of whom he sought information, had plainly been on this spot very recently. He had smoked one cigarette fully and, for some reason, had cast away another hardly smoked. Since Dacers had not encountered him in the street, he reasoned he was inside the building, possibly conferring with the artist, Crayford.

Dacers entered Marlborough Dwellings, climbed the stair remembering that young Melbourne said Crayford lived at number two just up the stair. Just as he reached the top of the stairs and had a good view of the corridor, a man came out one of the first doors, hastily. He was well dressed, had an olive cast of skin and carried a long wooden box. His whole demeanour was furtive and Dacers noticed that the door of the room he had just left was slanted on its hinges as if it had been forced.

The man with the box looked at Dacers, surprised. Then his expression turned hostile as he saw that Dacers was blocking the narrow stairway. To Dacers who had a long acquaintance with criminal types, everything about him was manifestly suspicious.

'Mr. O, sometimes called Owl?' asked Dacers.

O made a meaningless grunting sound. He was terrified of encountering the two dangerous Americans to whom he had revealed the whereabouts of the box nor did he wish to encounter police who might be investigating the theft from Birkenhead. On top of the fear of the Americans came the panicky notion that this lean, side-whiskered and lithe-bodied fellow who was so effectively blocking the stairway might well be a plainclothes peeler.

Dacers stepped up and stood just several steps down from the corridor's level. 'Mr. O, or Owl?' he repeated. 'I'd like a word or two with you.' To O, it was exactly the style of language a policeman might use and it brought a snarling answer from him.

'Get out of my way, damn you!' His face was a mixture of fear, anger and something else, a sort of deep-rooted greed which was also expressed in the possessive way in which he clutched the wooden box with its brass clasps. He wanted that box. He held it close to him, determined that no one would take it from him.

Dacers' thoughts began to race, trying to make sense of this man and the circumstances in which he encountered him. The condition of the the apartment door suggested that the man had forced it and had stolen the box. Now he was trying to make a quick getaway with it. He clutched it like a miser grasping his gold. Anger blazed in his eyes and he suddenly aimed a vicious kick at Dacers. Positioned on a lower stair, Dacers found it easy to grasp his foot and yank it forward. O fell backwards and landed flat on his back on the corridor floor. The box flew from his grasp, narrowly missed Dacers' head, smote the uncarpeted stairway and skittered down it.

O scrambled up from his lying position and lunged forward down the stairs in a blind effort to recover the box and barged into Dacers, flailing with his fists, trying to get past him. Dacers grasped O around the waist with both hands and, locked together, grunting and panting, they began to fall down the stairs. Just as they neared the box on the bottom stair, O planted a knee forcibly in Dacers' groin.

A gurgle of pain gusted out of Dacers and he released his grip on O who slithered down towards the box. He grasped it even before he was on his feet then began to stagger to a standing position. Dacers, winded, was grasping the rickety banister rails and hauling himself up from the grubby treads of the stairs. Down in the entrance hall of the tenement building, he could see O making unsteady progress towards the street doorway, again clutching the box close to him.

Dacers fought against the pain in his groin and began to stumble down into the entrance hall with the notion that he could leap on O's back before he went through the street door. Then he saw O freeze on the upper step of the entrance at the sight of three men coming up the steps of Marlborough Dwellings—two of them were the pair of Americans who had terrified him in Putney the day before. Their companion had a similar transatlantic look about him and he limped, dragging the toes of one foot as he walked.

Dacers, too, froze at the sight of these newcomers. Two he recognised as the orator of the meeting at Cremorne Gardens and his companion. The third, most startling of all, was his bearded would-be murderer of the smart disguise who had disguised his limp by riding a horse. He was now without his beard but Dacers was in no doubt as to his identity. He could clearly see the large, distinguishing wart on his face.

With lightning speed, a drama began to be acted out even as Dacers set foot in the entrance hall.

The newcomers were face-to-face with O, who snapped out of his paralysis of fear and began to run down the steps to the street. The man who had addressed the Cremorne meeting, yelled: 'By God, it's O—and with the box!'

O was now running along Thistle Street, still clutching the box. Naked fear was causing him to overcome his fatigue after his tussle on the stairs and he was running blindly, intent only on getting clear of the men who menaced him.

'I'll get him!' hooted the man from Cremorne whom Dacers recalled his companion introducing as a sergeant-major. His hand came out of his topcoat pocket flourishing a revolver. His companion, the orator from Cremorne yelled an objection and grabbed him by his shoulder at the very moment he fired at the retreating O. The bullet screamed wide of him but it caused the terrified O to drop the box just as a second mis-fired shot exploded behind him inspiring him to pump his legs yet more energetically. The box forgotten, every fibre of his being was aching to be out of this situation. He saw the opening of an alley, a mere crack between a couple of mean, slanted structures, and he fled into it.

On the steps of Marlborough Dwellings, the responsible Lewis Sadler was restraining Jefferson Dobbs. 'You damned fool,' he growled. 'How many times do I have to tell you that shooting in this country can only bring trouble?' He pushed the impetuous Dobbs against the side of the large entrance doorway. 'Put that gun back in your pocket and leave it there,' he ordered.

Septimus Dacers was lurching across the entrance hall, intent on reaching this threesome of newcomers. He wanted to get his hands on the third man, the limping one who had tried to kill him and was in the act of trying to sneak away while his American companions were arguing. The entangled affair of the box and the devious Mr. O, of which Dacers had no detailed knowledge was forgotten. He only saw the man who had worn a false beard attempting to slip down the steps of Marlborough Dwellings and into the street.

Dacers was dimly aware that the staircase behind him was filling up with shocked and inquisitive people, residents of Marlborough Dwellings' modest apartments, some of whom had obviously been roused from their beds. They were possessed by collective alarm and a panic was spreading among then. *'There were shots!'* called one jittery voice: *'Is it the Fenians?'*

The notion of armed insurrectionists being loose in no-account little Thistle Street took hold among residents of nearby dwellings who had tumbled into the street at the sound of shooting. *'The Fenians! It's the Fenians!'* shouted one voice after another. *'The Fenians!'* screeched a distraught woman. *'It's the damned Irish Fenians come to murder us all!'*

Dacers was acting almost in a world seeming to be detached from true reality: he had barged his way out of Marlborough Buildings and seized Ned Grandon by the shoulders just as he stepped down to the pavement, ready to launch himself into limping flight. Sadler and Dobbs ceased their arguing abruptly, realised with astonishment that the man who had accompanied the disguised girl in the flight through Cremorne Gardens was among them and handling the treacherous Grandon with whom they wanted to deal in their own way. They forgot their argument and closed in on Dacers belligerently.

'Stand back!' shouted Dacers loudly. 'This man attempted murder and I'm making a citizen's arrest. I call on all here to assist!' A tenement of Marlborough Dwellings' character naturally sheltered some who were hostile to the police but there was a surge of activity on the stairs as numerous individuals descended to the hallway.

Young Adolphus Crayford was just walking into one end of Thistle Street at that moment having made an early start on a long trudge to a cheapjack publishing house to collect more prepared plates for more penny dreadful illustrations. He had to halt on the pavement to allow a heavy police van, hauled by a pair of lathered horses go rushing by with clattering hooves and rumbling iron-rimmed wheels. It thundered into Thistle Street where Crayford could see a number of people outside Marlborough Dwellings. Full of curiosity, he walked towards the place he called home and watched the police van stop outside it. Its rear door flew open and a number of top-hatted peelers spilled out. He could see that a number carried bulldog pistols.

Meantime, the fleeing O found that the alley into which he ran, led him into a littered alley running behind shops in Southampton Row. He hastened along it until he found an outlet between two shops that led him into Southampton Row. Leaning against a wall, he recovered his breath. Then he saw a cabstand with a hansom waiting alongside it and he hurried towards it.

'Where to, sir?' called the cabbie from his high seat. O thought of some crowded place where he might hide himself in a throng until he gathered his wits fully.

'Euston Railway Terminus', he stipulated. So, Mr. O, the chickaleery bloke, the veritable box of smart tricks, rode away from a venture that had gone badly wrong, leaving the box that he believed contained something of fabulous value lying on the cobbles of a mean street. Still, he told himself, there would be other chances of audacious villainy and he would rise again. He would have to lie low for a time, dodging the police. He was marrying soon and that would mean a change of abode. He would fade away as he had done before, but he would most assuredly be back!

At Marlborough Dwellings, there was a press of humanity crowding the entrance and a good number of those present were policemen with ready bulldog pistols. Their leader was a heavy set man in a long top coat with frogged braiding across its chest. His choker collar bore the insignia of a street patrol inspector embroidered in silver thread.

'What's going on here?' he shouted in a stentorian North Country accent. 'We're from Southampton Row police station. We heard a couple of shots from this way and somebody said the Fenians had shown up—' He broke off, seeing a struggling knot of men at one corner of the entrance steps. There, Sadler and Dobbs were trying to manhandle the hapless Ned Grandon away from Septimus Dacers and several others who had come to his aid. Fists were flying energetically. The police inspector waded into the melee, cuffing ears and thumping heads to break up the struggle then he detailed several of his men to watch the participants.

He recognised Dacers who emerged bruised from the thick of the battle.

'Why, Mr. Dacers! You remember me, Jack Tomlinson? I was with Inspector Twells and yourself in that affair of the Swell Mob and the stolen jewels. What's the row here? I hear American accents flying around. Are some of these people the ex-American soldiers who've come over to make Fenian trouble?'

'I do indeed remember you, Inspector,' panted Dacers. 'No, this has nothing to do with the Fenians, but I want this man arrested for attempted murder.' He indicated Ned Grandon. 'I'll give you information later.'

'Sergeant Simpson, put the bracelets on this man and keep a close watch on him and I want everyone involved in this row rounding up,' stipulated the inspector. 'Mr. Dacers, if you're alleging attempted murder, you'll need to make statements at the station.'

A constable approached him carrying the wooden box retrieved from the street. 'Found it outside, sir,' he reported. 'It seems someone from here was running away with it.'

'Really?' rumbled the inspector. 'Stolen property?'

'Yes, Inspector. It is very much stolen property. It was stolen from someone of great note,' said a firm female voice accented with the soft touch of the Southern States of America.

Dacers whirled around and his jaw dropped when he saw Roberta Van Trask pushing her way through the thinning group of people in the entrance hall. The soldierly form of Richard, her father's coachman hovered behind her.

She smiled at Dacers but concern showed in her eyes. 'Mr. Dacers, you've been fighting and you seem to have a black eye. Are you all right?'

Utterly bewildered, Dacers gasped: 'I'm quite all right. But what are *you* doing here?'

'I wanted to be involved in the matter you were chasing up, remember? You told me the full address you were going to in order to inquire after Mr. O and I'd be a very poor detective if I couldn't accurately memorise an address, don't you think?' She gave him a heart-warming and sweetly disarming smile. 'Father doesn't mind me displaying the Van Trask pioneering spirit of adventure, so I persuaded Richard to bring me here. It seems I missed all the fun.'

For the first time, he fully took in the cut of her skirt. Shorter than a crinoline, it was spread out and apparently wired only at the sides, where the crinoline had a vast under-framework. It plainly allowed the wearer much more freedom.

'What on earth is that garment?' he asked.

'Don't you ever read the fashion notes? This is the crinolette, the up-to-the minute successor to the crinoline. It will be exactly the garment to suit our policewoman—when the government comes to its senses and permits such things as policewomen!'

Inspector Tomlinson's men had restored quiet to the hallway of Marlborough Dwellings, Sergeant Simpson and a couple of constables guarded the handcuffed Ned Grandon as well as Sadler and Dobbs, Dacers having remarked that their role in England might bear investigation.

The Inspector held the long wooden box and noted that its brass locks had been damaged probably through the ill usage of being dropped down the stairs or dropped in the street. They looked as if they might easily be opened.

Roberta approached Tomlinson. 'I think you'll find that object belongs to the United States, Inspector,' she said. 'My father is on the staff of the embassy in Grosvenor Square and he and Ambassador Adams know all about it.'

'Sorry, Miss. I can't release it,' said Tomlinson. 'It could be evidence and must be taken to the station, but I'll tell my superiors your embassy might have a claim on it. There's no reason why it can't be opened to verify its contents if those locks can be forced.'

Near the entrance to the building, Sadler, Dobbs and even Grandon strained their necks forward, eager to know what was contained in this box which had figured so dramatically in their lives. Tomlinson, Dacers and Roberta attempted to wrench the lid of the box open. The task proved stubborn until Tomlinson produced a big pocket knife and levered the damaged locks. The lid opened up. Inside, there was a faded length of stoutly woven fabric, wrapped around what was probably a length of pole. The fabric was discoloured, seemingly by exposure to much varied weather and sea spray. A large star on a broad band was plainly visible as part of the flag's red white and blue design.

'A Confederate flag!' declared Roberta.

She found a square of vellum tucked into one side of the folded flag. It bore a legend in neat, professional calligraphy:

> *This is the flag of the Confederate States' commerce raider, 'Shenandoah', which never surrendered to the government of the United States at the close of the War Between the States, 1861-1865. The commander and crew, having been preying on United States' shipping in distant waters, did not know the war was over until six months after its close. Rather than surrender in an American port and face the charges of piracy threatened by the United States' government, they embarked on an epic voyage to Liverpool by way of Cape Horn, facing many difficulties which were heroically borne and tested their calibre as courageous American seamen. Their ultimate surrender was to the British authorities.*

From where he stood under police guard, Lewis Sadler, sometime sergeant-major in General Edmund Vavasour's Georgia Crackers, could not help uttering a heartfelt cry at what was revealed by this troublesome box which he and Dobbs had chased across many a mile: 'My God! A scrap of the old rebel flag—the Unconquered Banner!'

And Septimus Dacers formed his lips into a tight line, thinking his own thoughts. It was from the unconquered rebel ship Shenandoah, the man calling himself 'Mr. Fortune', founder and cunning criminal brain of the Dixie Ghosts, had slipped ashore at Liverpool to work mischief.

CHAPTER 14

SYMBOLS

Dacers, spruced up and looking like a man intent on a vital course of action in spite of sporting a black eye, presented himself at the front door of Theodore Van Trask's home yet again. The butler, Frederick, opened the door and made no attempt to hide his smile on seeing Dacers.

'Miss Roberta will definitely see you, sir.' He intoned. His usual stone face melted into an un-butler-like grin when he noted the black eye. Dacers entered rather nervously, seeming to have something on his mind.

It was the morning after the showdown at Marlborough Dwellings. Dacers had spent the previous evening at Southampton Row police station with Inspector Jack Tomlinson, his superiors and Sadler and Dobbs. Ned Grandon, as one due to face criminal charges, was held in a cell. Dacers made a Statement concerning Grandon's shooting attempt and, from Sadler and Dobbs, came the full story of their orders from General Vavasour to seek the box—for which he had an almost religious obsession. They told of their task of rallying support among surviving Southern supporters in Europe for his high-flown dream of returning Georgia into British hands. Possession of the flag of the *Shenandoah,* was simply a symptom of the old man's desire for a symbolic relic of his dream of the unconquered banner. Whatever happened to his beloved Georgia in future, it should never be forgotten that Georgians once stood together under the rebel colours and made enormous sacrifices for what they called freedom. It was Vavasour's hope that at some time, in the future in the new Georgia he hoped to create, the *Shenandoah's* unconquered banner would be given a place of honour.

At the close of the interviews, the chief superintendent in charge, stroked his ample beard and indicated Sadler and Dobbs. 'I can't see that these men are answerable to any of our laws. Of course, they pursued this box thing which we know to have been stolen but they never found it, so they can't be accused of handling stolen property. They seem only to have followed an illogical dream, but that is no crime. People the world over do that every day. Matters don't rest with me, of course. This is the sort of thing that will be settled by people higher than myself.'

Roberta received Dacers in the familiar ante-room and she, too noted his unusual nervous demeanour. She ordered tea for both of them and listened intently as he told her of the proceedings at the police station.

At the end, she laughed. 'Poor Mr. Dacers—was there never any mention of prosecuting whoever gave you that beautiful black eye? But I have news for you. My father told me that, early this morning, a government messenger brought word to Mr. Adams that the two men from Georgia will not be proceeded against but they are not here to do any good, so they will be deported. The third man will be charged with the attempted murder of yourself. And the flag affair has been settled. It was found to be historic property of the United States and will be given into Mr. Adams' keeping. Father told me that Mr. Adams will exercise his discretion and return it to its owner in Birkenhead who, as you know, is an American honoured by both North and South and, indeed, by the whole world.'

She paused, smiled enigmatically and said with some feeling: 'That flag and its box were mere symbols. In fact, this whole affair seems to have been about symbols but then, maybe that was fitting. Symbols and gestures turn up throughout the whole of our Civil War. A young officer of a volunteer regiment who has never yet heard an angry shot rushes off to the photographer in his new uniform and has likeness taken as he poses with his hand thrust into the breast of his tunic like Napoleon. A symbol of his determination to make history on the battlefield. A youthful soldier falls face down in action and pleads with his comrades to lift him and turn him about so his family will know he died facing the enemy. Symbols and gestures, Mr. Dacers. Do they really have any worth?'

Dacers shuffled his feet and gave a nervous cough. Then he took the plunge.

'Miss Van Trask—Roberta,' he began huskily, 'I am not a wealthy man and I am unlikely ever to be able to offer you a fortune in gold. The most precious thing I can offer is a total, unswerving devotion so long as I have a breath in my body. You spoke of gestures and symbols. Well, even if I am scorned and laughed at, I came here to make a specific, old time gesture.'

Her face which had considered him with an expression of wonderment was transformed by a spreading, radiant smile and her remarkably expressive eyes sparkled with affection.

'A gesture, Mr. Dacers?' she queried.

'Yes—this gesture.' He stood up, moved a little nearer her chair and made an elaborate show of going down on one knee and placing his right hand over his heart.

Roberta began to chuckle then said: 'Oh. Mr. Dacers—dear, shy, reticent Englishman that you are—*I thought you'd never ask!*'

FIRST AFTERWORD

"THE PATHFINDER OF THE SEAS"…

Matthew Fontaine Maury became famous as "The Pathfinder of the Seas". It was a title richly earned by this American sailor, scientist and scholar who served in two navies, that of the United States and, after the outbreak of the Civil War, that of the rebel Confederate States. He did invaluable work and was a benefactor of seafarers the world over.

Born in Virginia in 1806, he entered the US Navy at eighteen as a midshipman. He had a short experience at sea before an accident left him with a leg injury that ruled out further seafaring. He remained in the navy and devoted himself to intense scholarship, studying navigation, winds, currents and the behaviour of the oceans and seas of all the world. He charted marine dangers in every part of the globe, investigated safe routes and published books that put him in the debt of naval men, merchant seamen and sea-goers of every description. In 1842, while the United States was still at peace, he was made Superintendent of the United States Naval Observatory but when the Southern States broke with the Union at the dawn of the Civil War, as a Virginian, he resigned his commission and joined the infant Confederate States Navy.

He was advised to go to England to help spread propaganda promoting support for the recognition of the Confederacy by European nations and to work with James D Bulloch, the South's chief naval naval agent in procuring and commissioning ships for the Southern navy. Although opposed to slavery, Maury, a devoted Christian, outspokenly desired an end to the devastating war between his countrymen. He nevertheless worked earnestly for a Southern victory and was responsible for procuring several ships in Britain and France. He settled in Birkenhead to where he managed to bring his wife and children.

In 1865 six months after the end of the Civil War, the Confederate commerce raider *Shenandoah* which was commissioned through the efforts of Bulloch and Maury, arrived in Liverpool. She had been prowling Arctic waters in search of US shipping, unaware that hostilities had ceased until meeting a British merchantman. Rather than surrender in an American port for fear of his crew being hanged as pirates, her commander, James Waddell, brought her on an epic voyage by way of Cape Horn to Liverpool where she was surrendered to the British authorities. It was the boast of her crew that they were the last to fly the battle flag of the Confederate States.

Soon afterwards, the *Shenandoah's* officers visited Maury and his family at Birkenhead and gave a number of souvenirs of the ship to Maury's daughters. The flag was presented to Miss Eliza Maury. For years, it was kept in secret for fear of its being seized by British customs authorities but, after the turn of the century, it was returned to the United States and lodged in the Confederate Museum in Richmond, Virginia, the former capital of the Confederate States.

In 1866, Matthew Maury left his family for a time, going to Mexico. Napoleon the Third, the grandiose Emperor of the French, had invaded that country and set up another Bonaparte, the Austrian Archduke Maximillian, as puppet emperor when he considered his conquest to be complete. Several noted Confederate military men and ex-politicians went to Mexico to enter Maximillian's service, rather than endure the rigours of Reconstruction in the defeated South.

Maximillian made Maury 'Imperial Commissioner for Immigration' and the Pathfinder of the Seas had hopes of bringing defeated Southerners to Mexico and setting up a colony called New Virginia.

After a short time, he returned to England to visit his family and while he was away, Mexican military force overthrew the rickety structure of Maximillian's empire. Maximillian, victim of the hare-brained French adventure, was imprisoned and, the following year, shot by firing squad. His wife, the tragic Empress Carlotta, lost her reason permanently.

Remaining in England, Maury earned honours from across the globe for his work for the benefit of the international maritime community. The British First Lord of the Admiralty, at a public dinner in his honour, gave him a substantial cash prize; the University of Cambridge made him an honorary Doctor of Laws; there was a valuable set of coins from Pope Pius XI and several countries conferred knighthoods or the equivalent on him.

In 1868, Maury and his family returned to the United States where, in his native State, he became a professor at Virginia Military Institute. He travelled, lecturing on scientific themes and made an important study of the natural history and future potential of Virginia, a State which saw the highest number of Civil War battles. Its aim was to restore the health of the State.

In 1873, the highly honoured Pathfinder of the Seas died, aged 77, at his home in Lexington, Virginia.

Any suggestion that the flag of the raider *Shenandoah* was stolen from Maury's Birkenhead home in 1867 must be put down to novelist's licence!

SECOND AFTERWORD
...AND THE MAN WHO DIED TWICE

One night in April 1890, a man was found lying close to a public house in Chelsea. He was said to be dead and his throat was cut. In his mouth there was a coin which some reports said was a sovereign while others claimed it was a half-sovereign. Later speculation about the presence of the coin in the mouth suggested it symbolised one guilty of slander while another opinion drew on mythology and recalled the way a corpse was equipped to pay the ferryman who took the soul across the River Styx.

The man was Charles Augustus Howell. He was 50 years old and he had a colourful life in which legend and blatant lies were entangled with much shady activity including unproven suggestions that he was a blackmailer.

Howell was born in Oporto, Portugal, of an English father and Portuguese mother whom he claimed had aristocratic origins. He frequently wore the ribbon of a Portuguese royal order which he said was conferred in perpetuity on her family. As a young man, he arrived in England from the Continent, supposedly after being caught cheating at cards.

Between 1858 and 1864, he was missing from England, according to his own tales, indulging in various European exploits. Among other things, he claimed he was an accomplice in the attempt to assassinate Napoleon III, Emperor of the French, for which his friend Felice Orsini, accused of throwing a bomb at the royal carriage, was executed.

Howell was closely associated with notables in the British art world in the 1860s and 1870s as an artists' agent, a dealer in objects of fine art and a fixer of various deals, astonishingly adept at buying and selling. In artistic circles, some relished his winning charm and glib, often outrageously transparent, tall tales but others could not stand him. The poet Algernon Charles Swinburne called him 'the vilest wretch I ever came across' and Whistler said of him: 'Criminally speaking, the Portugee was an artist.'

The Cockney mistress of one of the artists referred to him as "'Owell" thus he was given the nickname 'Owl.' By the time of his death, Howell had fallen on hard times.

Howell went down in legend as the man who organised and supervised the exhumation of the body of Lizzie Sidall, the wife of the painter and poet Dante Gabriel Rossetti, from her grave in Highgate Cemetery in 1869, seven years after burial. Rossetti wanted to retrieve a book of his unpublished, poems which he buried with her enfolded in her hair, so that he might publish them. He could not bring himself to attend the exhumation and stipulated that it must be done at dead of night and kept secret from the general public. Later, word of it got out, possibly through Howell.

Howell had an attractive, statuesque wife as well as a mistress, Rosa Corder, who bore him a daughter. She was an accomplished painter who had been a pupil of the pre-Raphaelite artist, Frederick Sandys. A scandal occurred when it was discovered that some drawings attributed to Dante Gabriel Rossetti were fakes and it was believed that they were created by Corder, acting under Howell's persuasion. This caused a split between Howell and Rossetti.

Very soon after reports of the finding of Howell's body were made public, another story became current. This said he was not dead when found but died later in the Home Hospital in Fitzroy Street—ironically a street long associated with London's artistic and literary colony. The cause of death was said to be pneumonic phthisis, a form of tuberculosis, and the wounds to his throat were for some reason caused surgically after death.

After his death it was found that Howell had hoarded a substantial set of letters from notables he was acquainted with and it was conjectured that he kept them for blackmail purposes but there was never any evidence of blackmail against him.

Curiously, no reports of an inquest or a police inquiry have ever surfaced, giving rise to a conspiracy theory around the death of 'Owl.'

Charles Augustus Howell inspired Arthur Conan Doyle to create Charles Augustus Milverton, the blackmailer in the Sherlock Holmes saga.

Any suggestion that Charles Augustus Howell ever organised a robbery at the Birkenhead home of Matthew Meary in 1867 must be put down to novelist's licence.

ABOUT THE AUTHOR

Anthony Arthur Glynn was born in Manchester in 1929, and had a disrupted wartime childhood including enduring the Luftwaffe's blitzing of the city in 1940 and 1941.

Drawn to art and writing from an early age, he was strongly influenced by two uncles, one a newspaperman who, in his spare time, wrote a variety of articles as well as fiction for juvenile weeklies. The other, who settled in Canada, was a chief theatrical scenic artist, working on the sets for many top stage shows.

Reading avidly from a young age, he became interested in all kinds of books and devoured popular fiction. Discovering the American comic strip *Buck Rogers* when he was about seven sparked off a lifelong interest in science fiction, and he later became well known among British science fiction fans. This activity led to lasting friendships and opportunities to write and illustrate in the amateur fanzines of Britain and the US.

At twenty-two came his first professional science fiction sale. Others followed and he worked in other fields, including juvenile fiction and, eventually, western and detective novels.

He started work as a textile designer in Manchester at sixteen and studied the subject at Manchester Regional College of Art in the evenings. After two years' National Service in the army, he changed direction for a short period, his fascination with theatre and film leading him into the professional film world—as a projectionist for the Rank Organisation.

In his early twenties, he became a reporter on a weekly newspaper in Cheshire, serving an enjoyable apprenticeship covering rural events and riding country lanes on a bicycle. Later, he returned to Manchester, produced some Western novels; worked on the features desk of the *Sunday Mirror* and spent thirty-three years with the *Bolton Evening News* newspaper group as chief reporter, then assistant editor of one of its weekly papers.

Since retiring, he has written a number of new western novels as well as short science fiction and fantasy stories for Wildside's *Fantasy Adventures* series. Currently he is planning on a return to detective fiction, and *Case of the Dixie Ghosts* and its sequel, *The Symbol Seekers*, reflects his interest in the strong links between Lancashire and America in the U.S. Civil War.

www.ingramcontent.com/pod-product-compliance
Lightning Source LLC
Chambersburg PA
CBHW020143180626
46810CB00004B/1702